Dorothy and Reading Help in Oz

(Featuring Dorothy Gale as a Mature Adult: Vol. V)

James L Fuller

Dorothy and Reading Help in Oz

(Featuring Dorothy Gale as a Mature Adult: Vol. V)

Written in 1996, revised in 2012

Copyright © 2012 by James L. Fuller

All rights reserved. No part of this book may be reproduced or transmitted in any form or by any means without permission in writing from the author. This includes electronic or mechanical means such as photocopy, recording, or any information storage and retrieval systems.

Fuller Publishing
Coos Bay, Oregon
Email: fullerpublishing@yahoo.com

Acknowledgments

I wish to thank Carolyn Owens and Violet Ogle for their suggestions on the plot of this story.

I wish to acknowledge that my drawings of stork, China Country, the Scarecrow and the Wizard are based on drawings by W. W. Denslow. The college singers and dancers are based on his Munchkin dancers.

I wish to acknowledge that my drawings Fuddlecumjig, Cuttenclips, the Sawhores, Ozma and Ozma II, Glinda and the Great Book of Records are based on drawings by John R Neill. My drawing of Fuddlecumjig mayor is based on a drawing of Uncle Henry by John R. Neill.

Dedication

I dedicate this book to all the adults who weren't able to learn to read well from their formal education. It is still not too late to learn to read!

Contents

Chapter		Page
1.	The New Airport	1
2.	The Flight to Lexington	6
3.	The Flight to Familyland	12
4.	The Thunderstorm	18
5.	A Surprise Visit to Ozma	23
6.	Off to The College	28
7.	China Country	33
8.	Fuddlecumjig	38
9.	Miss Cuttenclip	45
10.	The Athletic College of Oz	51
11.	Having Fun Reading and Spelling	57
12.	The Wizard Helps Katie	62
13.	Tommy's Spelling Problem	69
14.	The Wizard Helps Tommy	74
15.	Katie Practices Reading	79
16.	Plans For the Music Program	84
17.	The Wizard Helps Dr. Rob	89
18.	The Singing Demonstration	94
19.	Trying the Musical Instruments	99
20.	Try-outs for the Singing Groups	104
21.	Dr. Rob Reading Lesson	108
22.	The Music Director Lessons	113
23.	The College Orchestra	118
24.	Time for a Break	123
25.	The Drum Lesson	127
26.	The Trumpet Lesson	132
27.	Practice, Practice, Practice	136
28.	The Singing Competitions	141
29.	The Orchestra Concert	146
30.	Familyworld	150
31.	Familyland	155

Chapter 1 – The New Airport

It was the summer break from school and college. It had been a cold stormy spring term, in Eastern Kentucky. The term seemed like it would never end. Dorothy was taking her nephew Tommy, and niece Katie, on a trip to the amusement park Familyland for several days of fun. Aunt Dorothy is Dorothy Gale from Kansas.

Tommy and Katie's Dad, George Gilbert, dropped off Katie, Tommy, and their Aunt Dorothy at the new airport just outside of town. The new airport made it possible to catch a commuter airplane ride to one of the big city airports. This saved a six hour round trip by automobile to the nearest big city airport.

"Don't forget to call home after you arrive at your hotel," said George. "Dorothy! Did you remember to bring the medical release forms for Katie and Tommy? Have you got the power of attorney that makes you their guardian for the trip?"

"Yes, George!" answered Dorothy. "I have those papers right here in my purse. I also have our airplane tickets. You can go on to work. We will be just fine!"

"Okay!" replied George. "Good bye! Have a good trip!"

"Good bye," said Katie and Tommy together.

"Good bye," said Dorothy.

George got back into his car and drove off, headed for work. Dorothy, Katie, and Tommy waved goodbye to George.

Katie, Tommy and Aunt Dorothy picked up their luggage and carried it into the airport terminal building and up to the ticket counter. They were planning to take a commuter airplane to Lexington, Kentucky. There they would take a charter flight to Familyland in California.

Dorothy got their luggage checked in and the three of them went to the waiting room where they sat down to wait for the airplane. Katie and Tommy were excited about the trip. They had never been to Familyland. Tommy and Katie walked clear around the inside of the terminal building. They could hardly wait for their airplane to arrive.

While they were waiting, Dorothy saw one of her fellow college professors come into the airport terminal. It was Dr. Rob Patterns, a Professor of Music. After Dr. Rob had finished checking in his luggage, he came over to the waiting room.

"Hello, Dr. Patterns," greeted Dorothy. "What a surprise to see you here."

"Why hello, Dorothy," replied Dr. Patterns. "I didn't know you would be here."

"I'm taking my niece, Katie, and nephew, Tommy, on a trip to Familyland," continued Dorothy. She called Tommy and Katie over to her. "Katie and Tommy, this is Dr. Rob Patterns from the Music department at my college."

"Hello, Dr. Patterns," greeted Katie and Tommy.

"Hello, Katie and Tommy," replied Dr. Patterns. "Why don't you just call me Rob?"

"Hi, Rob," replied Tommy and Katie.

"Well, Rob," said Dorothy. "What brings you to our new airport?"

"Why I am taking the commuter airplane to Lexington. There I am catching a charter flight to Familyworld," replied Rob. "Some of the other music professors and I are going to Familyworld to present a show on Eastern Kentucky Folk Songs at the Folk Music Center."

"Since we are all taking the same airplane flight to Lexington," said Dorothy, "would you care to wait with us?"

"I would be happy to wait with you," answered Rob, as he took a seat next to them.

"Dr. Rob," said Tommy, "what musical instruments do you play?"

"Why I play the Banjo and the Piano," replied Rob. "I think all Music Professors are required to play a piano to some extent."

Katie asked, "How long have you played them?"

"I started trying to play the piano at about age three," replied Rob. "It wasn't until I was in middle school that I got a chance to try playing the banjo."

"Which of the instruments do you like best?" asked Tommy.

"I like the banjo best," replied Rob. "But I am also good with the piano! Do you two play any musical instruments?"

"Well, I can sing some and have played rhythm instruments in school," replied Tommy. "Our teacher even tried to teach us to read music, but I found that difficult to do."

"That's about the same for me," added Katie. "The sharps and flats are real confusing."

"You are still young," said Dr. Rob. "You may still decide to try playing some musical instrument. Reading music is much easier than reading a book."

"Now you know all about my interests," continued Dr. Rob. "What do you two like to do?"

"Well Tommy is really good at working with computers," said Katie. "And I like computers too!"

"We are also into Boy Scouts and Girl Scouts," added Tommy.

"What grades are you in at school?" asked Dr. Rob.

"I will be starting the sixth grade in the fall," replied Tommy.

"I'll be going into the fifth grade," replied Katie.

"How are you doing in school?" asked Dr. Rob.

"I am doing fine in most things," answered Tommy. "However I have trouble with spelling."

"Boy does he have trouble with spelling!" added Katie. "It was his spelling that almost kept him from coming on this trip!"

"And I suppose your reading skills didn't get you into trouble too," said Tommy. "You may be going into fifth grade, but you will still be reading at a third grade level!"

"Well, at least I didn't get caught cheating on a spelling test," said Katie.

"True," replied Tommy, "but Mother said they were thinking about holding you back a grade."

"Right!" answered Katie. "And they wanted to expel you."

"Now, Katie and Tommy," said Dorothy, "it is much too nice a day for fighting. Yes, you both have some problems in school, but I promised your mother that I would help you two out this summer. That's why you are still allowed to take this trip. Now let's just try to relax and have a little fun for a few days. After this trip, we will work on your spelling and reading problems!"

"You want to do the best you can at learning the fundamentals in school," added Dr. Rob. "After all, if you don't learn the fundamentals well, then you will have trouble for the rest of your lives. I've heard it said that if you do very poorly in some subject in school, then you will have to teach that subject as an adult. You don't want to grow up to be school teachers do you?"

"You mean I might have to teach children to spell when I grow up?" asked Tommy.

"And I might have to teach children to read?" added Katie.

"That would be awful," said Katie and Tommy together.

"Then you should give your Aunt your full attention this summer as she tries to help you!" finished Dr. Rob.

"Tommy and Katie are young and we have the whole summer," said Dorothy. "I am sure we can improve their reading and spelling skills by next fall."

"Do you two like music?" asked Dr. Rob of Tommy and Katie.

"Well, I do like many songs," replied Tommy. "I really enjoy singing around a campfire."

"I prefer music that one can dance to," answered Katie. "Singing is okay, but dancing is more fun. Singing and dancing is even better."

"Have you ever wanted to direct music?" asked Dr. Rob.

"Direct music?" questioned Tommy.

"You know, Tommy," replied Katie. "Like when you acting like you are the director or conductor of a band or orchestra."

"Oh yeah," said Tommy. "I think it would be fun to direct an orchestra."

"Right!" replied Katie. "You should see Tommy trying to conduct a band when no one is around. His arms are moving in all directions."

"And what about your attempts to dance?" added Tommy. "You don't exactly float through the air."

"Would you two like a quick lesson in directing music?" asked Dr. Rob.

"Sure!" replied Tommy.

"Okay!" said Katie.

"The first thing you need to do is look at is the time signature at the beginning of the sheet music," started Dr. Rob. "If it says it is 4/4 time, then you just move your arm like this." Dr. Rob took his right arm and went through 4/4 timing by first moving it down and saying one. Then he moved it diagonally up and to the right and said two. Next he moved straight across to the left and said three. Finally he moved it diagonally up, to the right and back to the starting point and said four. "Now you two try it!"

So Katie and Tommy tried moving their arms as directed while saying one, two, three and four. Their directing lessons had continued for several minutes, when they were interrupted by the public address system. It announced that the commuter airplane from Lexington was about to arrive. It would be unloading passengers shortly.

Katie and Tommy ran over to the windows looking out on the runway. There they saw the commuter airplane taxiing to the terminal building.

Chapter 2 – The Flight to Lexington

The commuter airplane was a small two engine turboprop airplane. It could only hold fourteen passengers. A turboprop is a jet engine that turns a propeller. While the airplane was taxiing up to the loading ramp, it made a loud roaring noise. Even inside the modern sound resistant airport terminal, the noise was very noticeable.

Katie and Tommy were watching the arrival of the airplane with intense interest. This was to be their first airplane ride. After the airplane came to a stop and shut down its engines, a door opened on it and steps unfolded down to the tarmac. Several passengers got off the airplane and came into the terminal. A motorized baggage cart moved out to the airplane. The luggage compartment under the airplane opened up and the luggage for the arriving passengers was removed from it and placed on the baggage cart. Next, the luggage for the departing passengers was loaded into the luggage compartment. Finally, the baggage cart returned to the airport terminal.

The public address system announced that the airplane flight to Lexington was now loading. Dorothy, Katie, Tommy, and Dr. Rob had to empty their pockets and take off their shoes and belts. Then they had to walk through a metal detector before they were allowed to leave the terminal building and go out to the airplane. Dorothy and Katie had to let their purses pass through an x-ray machine. Afterwards, they were all allowed to go to the airplane and climb aboard it. Inside the airplane, Katie and Tommy saw two rows of seven seats each down the two sides of the airplane. They sat in the front seats. From here, they could see into the cockpit and look at all the flight instruments. Dorothy sat behind Katie. Dr. Rob sat behind Tommy. Some other passengers sat behind Dorothy and Dr. Rob.

The pilot came aboard the airplane. She closed the door and locked it. The pilot greeted everyone and told them about fastening their seat-belts, where the emergency exits were located, and that this was a no smoking flight. As the only member of this flight crew, the pilot had to do everything. She walked past Katie and Tommy on her way to the cockpit.

The pilot turned on the fasten seat-belt sign and then started the engines. The sound from the engines started as a low frequency roar and then became higher and higher in frequency. It became louder and louder as the engines came up to full power. It was so noisy in the airplane that it was difficult to talk to one another.

With the increasing noise, both Katie and Tommy looked a little scared.

"Are all airplanes this noisy?" asked Katie in a very loud voice so she could be heard over the engine noise.

"Are you sure the propellers aren't going to fly off the engines?" asked Tommy.

"It's only this noisy during the take off," replied Dorothy. "This is a small airplane, so you are close to the engine noise. That's why the engines seem so noisy. The larger airplanes have noisier engines. But they also have better sound proofing and one sits further away from the engines."

The pilot released the breaks and started taxiing the airplane from the parking area out to the runway. Within a few moments, the runway was reached. The pilot then turned the airplane to point down the runway and set the breaks. There was another wait of two or three minutes. Finally the pilot brought the engines up to full power again. The airplane tried to move forward, but couldn't because the breaks were still on.

The brakes were released and the airplane started rolling down the runway. The engines screamed as the airplane gained speed. It only took two hundred yards before the airplane lifted off the runway. This was followed by two loud thumps as the landing gear retracted into the wings. The pilot pulled back on the control column and the airplane started to climb at a thirty degree angle. The airplane was still gaining speed. Dorothy, Katie, Tommy and Dr. Rob were pushed back into their seats by the acceleration of the airplane and the pull of gravity.

Tommy didn't want to think about what was happening so he decided to recall events of the last few days. It had only been a few days since his mother had the meeting with his teacher. Tommy's teacher had caught Tommy cheating on a spelling test. His mother was so upset by this news that she almost canceled Tommy's trip to Familyland.

"This is a very serious matter," continued the teacher. "We could even have Tommy expelled from school for such an action!"

"Why did you cheat on the spelling test?" asked Tammy, in front of his teacher. "How could you do such a thing?"

"I was afraid that I would fail the test," replied Tommy. "You worked so hard with me on studying for the spelling test, but I just couldn't seem to remember the words. I was afraid that you would be disappointed in me."

"Well, I am disappointed in you now!" responded Tammy. "What will your father say when he gets home?"

"It was the only way that I could think of for me to pass the test," continued Tommy. "You know that I have trouble with spelling. This was the last spelling test of the year. I thought that I could study spelling this summer. That way I would know the words by the next school year."

"But cheating on a test in school is really just cheating yourself out of a good education," added his teacher. "Covering up your lack of learning will just make your problem worse later."

"I know what I did was wrong and stupid," replied Tommy. "But I feel so helpless during spelling tests. I seem to do okay in the other subjects."

"Well, you need to work on your spelling skills this summer," said Tommy's teacher.

"I promise that we will do all that we can do to help Tommy with his spelling problem this summer," added Tammy.

"Would you mind giving me a list of the words that Tommy should be able to spell and use?"

"In that case, then I won't punish Tommy for trying to cheat this time," added his teacher. "But don't do it again. And yes, I can make you up a list of spelling words for Tommy."

Tommy and Tammy had walked quietly to their car. Neither of them spoke during the drive home.

Finally, when they turned into their driveway, Tammy said, "Tommy, if you will agree to work on your spelling this summer, I'll still let you go on the trip to Familyland with your Aunt Dorothy!"

"Thank you!" agreed Tommy. "Maybe Auntie Dorothy can give us some suggestions on where to start working on my spelling problem!"

Tommy's thoughts were interrupted when the airplane flew through some thunderstorm clouds.

The airplane began to pitch up and down. Katie began to wonder if this airplane flight to Familyland was going to be a treat or a punishment.

Katie, too, had been trying to avoid thinking about this airplane flight. She had been recalling events of the past week.

Only last week, Tammy had to visit Katie's teacher. It seems that Katie was reading at a full grade level below the grade she was in. Since reading is required for learning most other subjects in school, the teacher was worried about Katie and her reading skills.

Katie's teacher said to Tammy, "I think that we should hold Katie back a year. This will give Katie a chance to improve her reading skills!"

"But Katie is doing fine in all the rest of her schooling," objected Tammy. "Do you really think holding her back a year is necessary? Can't she work on her reading this summer? Perhaps she should attend summer school. Or we could get her a tutor?"

"Well, you are right about her doing fine in her other subjects," replied Katie's teacher. "Perhaps if you could get Katie to go to the public library and read one book a week, written for her grade level. Then have her do a book report to you on it. That should help she improve her reading. But she must work hard on it or she won't do well in school next fall!"

"Okay," agreed Tammy, "I agree to help Katie practice reading this summer and you will let her go on to the next grade. If she has trouble reading at the beginning of fall term, then her teacher can send her back to you for another year."

"Fine!" agreed Katie's teacher. "If you can improve Katie's reading skills this summer, she should do fine next fall."

Katie and Tammy had walked quietly out to the car. Once more there was no talking on the drive home.

Once at home, Tammy turned to Katie and said, "Katie, I don't know what I am going to do with you and Tommy. Tommy has spelling troubles and you have reading troubles. However, If you will let me, I'll try to help both of you this summer to improve your reading and Tommy' spelling. Maybe you can help each other?"

"So, does this mean the trip to Familyland is off?" asked Katie.

"No!" replied Tammy. "If you and Tommy will promise to work hard the rest of the summer, you can still go on the trip to Familyland with your Aunt Dorothy."

"I promise that I'll try hard to improve my reading," answered Katie. "It's not that I can't read, it's just that the teacher insists that I hold the book at a certain distance. But then sometimes I have trouble seeing the words."

"Well, your father and I will help you find out your problem and work on it this summer," stated Tammy. "Maybe your Aunt Dorothy can help you as well. You seem to like to visit her."

So the trip to Familyland was under way. The first leg on the commuter airplane had been noisy and bumpy. Another large bump brought Katie's attention back to the airplane flight.

"I sure hope this bouncing around stops soon," said Tommy.

"I second that vote," added Katie.

"Well, we should almost be to Lexington," replied Dorothy. "This bouncing around should stop soon."

About this time the airplane exited out of the other side of the thunderstorm clouds. The ride became much smoother. Soon the airplane started its descent into the Lexington airport.

Tommy and Katie watched with interest as the tiny houses and cars started to grow in size. They got bigger and bigger until they were almost life size. Then the airplane touched down at the Lexington airport.

The airplane taxied to the parking area and shut down its engines. Finally, everyone was allowed to get out of the airplane and walk to the airport terminal building. It was nice to be on solid ground once again.

Dorothy, Katie and Tommy said goodbye to Dr. Rob and went looking for the gate for the charter airplane to Familyland. Dr. Rob went looking for the charter airplane to Familyworld.

"I'm not so sure that I want to ride on a large airplane after the trip in the small airplane," said Tommy.

"That was a scary flight!" added Katie.

"Now don't worry," replied Dorothy. "The large airplanes ride much smoother than the little airplanes. Besides, the large airplanes can fly above the bad weather!"

Chapter 3 -- The Flight to Familyland

The Lexington airport was much larger than their home town airport. For one thing, the terminal building was several stories high. There were motorized loading ramps off of the two ends and center of the terminal building that allowed passengers to walk out the second story right into the cabin of the larger jet airplanes. These were called "Jet Ways." Large jet airplanes were parked at each of these Jet Ways.

As they walked from the commuter airplane to the terminal building, Tommy noticed how large the jet airplanes were in comparison with the commuter airplane.

"You are right, Auntie," said Tommy. "The jet airplanes are much larger than the commuter airplane. Are you sure they ride smoother than the commuter airplane?"

"And I hope they are a little quieter," added Katie. "It was difficult to hear each other on the commuter airplane."

"Yes, it will be quieter inside of the big jet airplane," replied Dorothy, "but it will still be a little noisy."

"So which one of these jet airplanes is the one going to Familyland?" asked Tommy.

"Well, it could be any of these airplanes or none of them," replied Dorothy.

"What?" responded Katie and Tommy together.

"It is still half an hour before our airplane is scheduled to leave," answered Dorothy. "Our airplane may not have landed yet. We need to go into the terminal and find out which gate our airplane leaves from."

They had to walk to the terminal building and walk up three flights of stairs to the passenger waiting area. They saw some of the commuter passengers being greeted by friends and then heading for the baggage claim area. The baggage area was downstairs along with a restaurant and several shops.

Dorothy, Katie and Tommy looked around the passenger waiting area for their gate to the airplane to Familyland. They found it at the far end of the terminal building. Katie and

Tommy ran over to the window and looked at the jet airplane that they were going to ride on. Finally, Tommy and Katie returned to Dorothy and sat down. They played games while they waited to board the airplane.

Dorothy checked the three of them in at the passenger check-in counter.

Finally, Dorothy said, "It is almost time to get on the airplane. You two should go use the restrooms." Katie and Tommy got up and walked to the restrooms. A few minutes later, they returned to the seating area where Dorothy was waiting for them.

Dorothy, Katie and Tommy boarded the airplane by walking out of the second story of the terminal building, through the Jet Way and on to the airplane. They found their seats and fastened their seat-belts. Just before the airplane took off, the Hostess went over the safety rules for their airplane.

The jet airplane took about ten minutes to disconnect the Jet Way and taxi out to the runway. It sat on the runway for several minutes. Finally, it took off. Within a few seconds, it increased its angle of accent and felt like it was going straight up. Then it reached its cruising altitude and leveled off.

Katie remarked, "The takeoff was even steeper than the one for the commuter airplane."

"You're right, Katie!" agreed Tommy. "That takeoff kind of takes one's breath away."

"Well, now we have leveled off," added Dorothy. "So let's just enjoy the rest of our flight."

Dorothy, Katie and Tommy watched the movie on their airplane flight. It was "Beaver Hollow." The movie ran for about one hour and twenty minutes.

After the movie ended, Tommy decided that he needed to use the restroom on the airplane. He walked to one of the restrooms in the tail of the airplane. Tommy entered that small restroom, shut and locked the door and tried to figure out how to use the facilities. The tail of the airplane was bouncing up and down as he is tried to do this. Finally, Tommy managed to complete his task and he returned to his seat, only slightly shaken up.

"Boy! The restroom is difficult to use," said Tommy to Aunt Dorothy. "Now I see why you wanted us to use the restrooms at the terminal. However, on a three hour flight, that may not be enough."

"Yes!" replied Dorothy. "Restrooms on an airplane are a challenge to use. I try not to have to use them!"

"You will never guess who I saw on the way back from the restroom," continued Tommy.

"Who did you see, Tommy?" replied Dorothy.

"Why I saw Dr. Rob Patterns sitting in the back of the airplane," answered Tommy. "I thought he was going to Familyworld?"

"He is going to Familyworld," answered Dorothy. "You must be mistaken. After all, this airplane is going to Familyland, in California. Familyworld is in Florida."

"I'm not mistaken," continued Tommy. "If you will come with me, I'll prove it to you."

Tommy led Dorothy to where Dr. Rob was seated. Dr. Rob was surprised to see Dorothy and Tommy.

"I didn't expect to see you two again," said Dr. Rob. "I thought you were going to Familyland."

"We are going to Familyland," replied Dorothy. "We thought you were going to Familyworld."

"But I am going to Familyworld," replied Dr, Rob.

"This airplane is headed for the Orange County airport in California," stated Tommy. "Isn't Familyworld in Florida?"

"Well, yes it is," answered Dr. Rob. "Don't tell me I got on the wrong airplane?"

"It certainly looks that way," said Dorothy. "At this point, there isn't much you can do about it until we land. Why don't you come and sit with us? Maybe we can think of a solution to your problem."

So Dr. Rob accompanied Dorothy and Tommy back to their seats. After they sat down, Tommy asked, "How does one get on the wrong airplane?"

"Well, I'm not sure what happened," replied Dr. Rob. "But I didn't pack my reading glasses, so I must have misread the signs."

"Well don't feel too bad," encouraged Tommy. "The flight attendant must have also misread your ticket."

"Why don't we compare our airplane tickets to your ticket, Dr. Rob," suggested Katie.

So Dorothy and Dr. Rob got out their tickets and compared them. The tickets were the same color, by the same airline and had almost identical printing on them. The only real difference was in the words 'Familyland' versus 'Familyworld'.

"Boy those tickets look identical to me," said Katie.

"Well, they are almost identical," agreed Dorothy. "They only differ in the words 'Familyland' and 'Familyworld'. So we can understand why a busy flight attendant might mistake one ticket for the other ticket."

"Okay," agreed Tommy. "I can see where you might have trouble reading the ticket without your reading glasses, but you do have the right ticket for Familyworld. It wasn't the ticket that you misread. It was the gate sign. You don't use reading glasses to read a gate sign."

"Tommy!" scolded Dorothy. "Mind your manners. You shouldn't talk to an adult like that."

"Bu-ut-t," stuttered Tommy. "It's true that Dr. Rob has a reading problem!"

"Tommy!" added Dorothy. "I don't want to tell you again. You shouldn't say such a thing."

"But, I am right!" continued Tommy.

"Tommy!" stated Dorothy. "It is not nice for children to find fault with adults. Sometimes children should just keep quiet."

"What happened, Tommy, was that I got careless," explained Dr. Rob. "You see I was in the coffee shop downstairs in the airport and I lost track of the time. Then I heard them announcing the final boarding call for the airplane to Familyworld. So I put down the pie and coffee that I was eating and ran upstairs to the airplane gates. I saw them closing the gate that I thought was my airplane to Familyworld. So I ran up to the ticket agents and handed them my ticket. They tore off part of my ticket and gave me a boarding pass. I ran through the Jet Way and just managed to get aboard the airplane before they could close the door."

"Now see, Tommy!" said Dorothy. "Dr. Rob gave you a logical reason for his being on our airplane. I think you owe Dr. Rob an apology!"

"I'm sorry, Dr. Rob," said Tommy.

"That's okay, Tommy," replied Dr. Rob. "No real harm done."

"So you do know how to spell Familyworld?" questioned Katie.

"Katie!" said Dorothy. "Enough is enough!"

"How about I just read the spelling off of my ticket," answered Dr. Rob. He then read, "F-A-M-I-L-Y-W-O-R-L-D. Does that sound correct?"

"I guess so," replied Katie.

"Fine, that is enough!" said Dorothy. "So let's change the subject!"

"Okay!" replied Tommy and Katie together.

"What did you think of the movie?" asked Tommy.

"It was very informative," replied Dr. Rob. "I always enjoy nature movies." So Dorothy and Dr. Rob continued to talk about the movie.

Meanwhile, Tommy and Katie put their heads together and whispered to each other for a couple of minutes. Then they got out a piece of paper and a pencil and started to print a note to Dr. Rob. When they finished writing the note, they folded it over and put Dr. Rob's name on the outside of it.

"Tommy! Katie! What have you two been up to?" asked Dorothy.

"We've been writing Dr. Rob an apology," said Katie.

"Would you be so kind as to hand it to Dr. Rob for us?" asked Tommy. "We hope that we spelled everything correctly!"

Dorothy passed the note to Dr. Rob.

Dr. Rob opened the note. He saw his name at the top of the page and Katie's and Tommy's names at the bottom of the page. The note started with, "We are sorry that . . ."

Dr. Rob put the note in his pocket and said, "Katie and Tommy, I accept your apology!"

"Would you mind showing Auntie Dorothy our apology note?" asked Katie.

"Why no!" replied Dr. Rob. He then took the note out of his pocket and handed it to Dorothy.

"Auntie!" said Tommy. "Would you read and check my spelling on the note? After all, we want to improve my spelling this summer."

Dorothy opened the note. She began reading: "Dear Dr. Rob. We are sorry that we upset you by saying that you have a reading problem. But as your friends, it is necessary that we tell you that we all know you do have a reading problem. . ."

At this point, Dorothy opened her eyes wide in surprise. Finally Dorothy said, "Tommy and Katie, I think you spelled every word correctly!"

"So we're all friends again?" asked Tommy. "I really did enjoy the music conducting lesson!"

"Yes, we are all friends again," replied Dr. Rob. "And I enjoyed teaching you how to conduct music."

"And our printing was big enough so that you could read the note without your reading glasses?" asked Katie.

"Yes, I could read the entire note," replied Dr. Rob. "Your printing was well done!"

"Would you mind reading the note out loud?" asked Tommy.

"I would prefer not to," replied Dr. Rob.

"One thing, Dr. Rob!" said Katie. "Friends don't go around lying to each other."

"While the note was an apology," added Tommy. "It also said we know you have a reading problem!"

"Tommy!" said Dorothy. "We are finished with this subject!"

"Actually, Tommy is right, Dorothy," said Dr. Rob. "I do have trouble reading."

"That's okay," added Tommy. "Katie has trouble reading and I have trouble spelling. We almost didn't get to come on this trip because of our problems."

"But Dr. Rob did get to come on this trip because of his reading problem," added Katie. "If he hadn't misread the gate sign, he would be on his way to Familyworld right now."

"Come to think about it," recalled Dorothy, "I don't ever remember you having your reading glasses with you at the college. You always get someone to read the memorandums to you."

"All right," confessed Dr. Rob. "You are right Dorothy. I don't need reading glasses. I can see everything just fine. I don't really have a reading problem. The problem is that I simply can't read!"

"What?" said Katie and Tommy together.

"Well, that does explain a lot of things," responded Dorothy.

Chapter 4 -- The Thunderstorm

"I don't quite believe you, Dr. Rob," said Tommy. "You have a Doctor of Philosophy in Music, and yet you say you can't read."

"Now that is an interesting statement," added Katie. "Perhaps Dr. Rob does read some?"

"Well, I can read my own name," replied Dr. Rob. "And I can even read numbers and music. However, I can't read books or even memorandums."

"But how did you get through school without being able to read?" asked Katie. "My school is threatening to hold me back a grade if my reading doesn't improve."

"How did you get through college," added Tommy.

"And I am sure graduate school must have been 'fun' if you couldn't read," said Dorothy.

"Well, getting through the public school wasn't that hard," began Dr. Rob. "I am a very good listener, and I have the ability to remember word for word what is said to me. I am almost a tape recorder. The hardest part was getting around taking written tests. However, if I would just show enough test anxiety, then I could usually get the teacher to give me an oral test. Those tests were easy for me."

"You remember everything that is said to you?" asked Tommy. "That makes learning easy!"

"Yes, I remember everything that is said to me," replied Dr. Rob. "For example, since we first met at our home town airport, our conversations have been as follows: . . ." Then Dr. Rob repeated word for word what Dorothy, Katie, Tommy and he had said to each other.

"Wow!" remarked Katie. "You really do remember everything that is said to you."

"In college I always joined study groups and discussion groups," continued Dr. Rob. "That way, I didn't have to read the textbook! I also took part in class discussion so that the teacher would know that I knew the material. That saved me from some bad test grades, on the few occasions where I couldn't dodge a written test. Fortunately, most of those tests were multiple choice tests!"

"I like multiple choice tests," said Katie. "They always have the right answer included in the question."

"I had to get other people to type up papers for me," said Dr. Rob. "I would either dictate the paper to them as they typed it or I would tape-record the paper."

"So you learned all the information," said Katie. "However somehow you just never learned to read."

"That about covers my story," said Dr. Rob. "My graduate work in music was fairly easy, since much of it was listening to and playing musical instruments."

"But isn't it hard to get along in our world without being able to read?" asked Katie. "I mean, how do you order at a restaurant? How do you know what is on television or what movie is playing?"

"How do you read a road map? Or for that matter how did you get a driver's license?" added Tommy.

"How do you use a telephone book or order things from a catalog?" asked Dorothy. "How do you shop at a grocery store? I bet writing a check must be a problem!"

"At restaurants, I always order from the specials," replied Dr. Rob. "The waiter or waitress always tells you what is in the specials. That way, I don't have to read the menu."

"I find things on the television by channel surfing and by remembering when and where I last saw that program," continued Dr. Rob. "When it comes to road maps, I can't read them. But I am not alone in that. Over half of the adult population of the United States can't read road maps!"

"Getting a driver's license does not require that one know how to read," stated Dr. Rob. "Oh, you do have to know the meaning of traffic signs, but those can be memorized. The driving inspector is allowed to read questions to a person who has a problem reading. It is just another case of my forgetting my reading glasses!"

"I can't order things from catalogs," finished Dr. Rob. "When it comes to shopping at a grocery store, I only buy things where I can see the actual product. I try to pay cash for things. However, the credit card and debit card makes it so I don't have to write a check at a store. You are right in that I can't write out the words for the amount of a check. If I have to use a check, I get someone else to write it for me. Then I just have to sign it!"

"Wow!" replied Katie and Tommy together.

"It actually sounds like it might be easier to learn to read than to have to get around reading all the time," said Dorothy.

"Dr. Rob, have you considered getting help with your reading problem? There are several organizations that exist just to help adults learn to read."

"Well, I have thought about getting help with my reading problem," replied Dr. Rob. "But then I would have to let people know that I can't read. After all the time I have spent trying to keep people from knowing about my problem, I am afraid of what they would think of me if they were to find out! They would probably think that I am dumb or just stupid! This would be especially true for all the strangers."

"I guess I was lucky to get caught cheating on the spelling test the first time that I tried cheating," replied Tommy. "I can still try to fix my problem before it controls my whole life!"

"Yes, Tommy," said Dr. Rob. "You are young and can still do something about your problem. Yes, you are lucky to have your problem known so soon!"

"Actually, Dr. Rob," added Dorothy. "Even you can still get help for your reading problem! If you do, it will make your life a lot easier. You are a very intelligent adult and it is still possible for you to overcome your reading problems."

"I don't know," replied Dr. Rob. "What would all my friends think if they knew I can't read? They would think I am a fool. No! I think I will just keep things as they are. That is if I can count on you to keep my secret?"

"We won't tell," said Tommy and Katie, together. "But you shouldn't tell people about our problems either!"

"What about you, Dorothy?" asked Dr. Rob.

"Your problems are your own business," replied Dorothy. "I won't tell other people about your problem. However, if you change your mind about wanting help, I am here to help you."

"Thank you, Katie, Tommy, and Dorothy!" replied Dr. Rob. "That takes a load off my mind. Now if we can just figure out how to get me to Familyworld."

"I think all you need to do is go talk to someone at the ticket counter when we land," suggested Dorothy. "I am sure that you are not the first person to ever get on the wrong airplane."

"I think you are right, Dorothy," said Dr. Rob. "Now does anyone know where we are?"

About this time, the pilot turned on the public announcement system and said, "Ladies and gentlemen, we are about to cross over the Rocky Mountains. There seems to be some thunderstorm activity ahead of us. Please remain in your seats and keep your seat-belts fastened."

The airplane then began to buck up and down. As time passed the up and down motion intensified. Lightening started to flash outside the airplane windows. Loose hand luggage, pillows, coats and anything else that wasn't tied down, went bouncing about the cabin of the airplane. People started using the air sick bags. Everyone was feeling a little motion sick.

"I thought you said these large jet airplanes could fly above the storms and don't bounce around?" questioned Tommy of his Auntie Dorothy.

"Well, they usually are able to fly above the storms," replied Dorothy. "But this storm may just be too big to get above or around. These large jet airplanes don't bounce around near as badly as the little commuter airplanes."

"Then I am glad we are in this big jet airplane," added Katie, "because this storm is really bouncing this big airplane around. I hope it doesn't get any worse."

About this time, the airplane started rising very rapidly. Everyone was pushed down in their seats. It seemed like the airplane kept rising forever. Would the airplane ever stop rising?

Then, without warning, the airplane started falling very rapidly. The few persons who hadn't fastened their seat-belts were lifted out of their seats. The lightning flashed more often. Then the lights went out inside of the airplane. The lightning flashed so brightly that all anyone could see for a few seconds was a white spot.

Katie and Tommy were scared. Everyone on the airplane was scared. It was not an enjoyable experience! How much more could the airplane and passengers take?

Chapter 5 -- A Surprise Visit to Ozma

The next thing Dorothy, Katie, Tommy, and Dr. Rob knew, they had fallen flat on the floor. The floor was covered with a thick rug, so no one was hurt. Slowly they came to realize that they were no longer on the jet airplane.

"Well, it's about time you were coming around," said a familiar voice.

"Ozma, is that you?" asked Dorothy.

"And just who did you think it was?" replied Ozma.

"If that is Ozma I hear," said Tommy, "then I don't think we are on the airplane anymore."

"I don't think we are in the United States anymore," added Katie.

"Then where in the world are we?" asked Dr. Rob.

"I believe we are in the Land of Oz," replied Dorothy. "The person standing in front of you, wearing that wide jeweled belt is Ozma, the ex-ruler of the Land of Oz. That's Glinda the Good, standing next to her. I think we are at Glinda's Palace, in her private chamber. That's the 'Great Book of Records' on the ebony stand."

"What do you mean by, 'we are in the Land of Oz'?" asked Dr. Rob. "Everyone knows there isn't any such place as the Land of Oz. It is only a make-believe place found in children's stories!"

"Then I don't suppose you want to know that Auntie Dorothy is a Princess of Oz," added Katie.

"Why do adults have so much trouble believing in the Land of Oz?" asked Tommy.

"We were just reading about your fun airplane ride," said Ozma. "And we thought you could use a few moments of peace and quiet."

"I, for one, was starting to feel a little air sick," replied Katie. "Thank you for bringing us here."

"I thought the ride was fun!" said Tommy. But his face had still not regained its normal color.

"What happened to the airplane?" asked Dorothy.

"The airplane will land safely with no serious injuries," replied Glinda. "Dorothy, Katie and Tommy will get to Familyland okay."

"What about me?" asked Dr. Rob.

"Who is this man?" asked Glinda.

"I don't know," replied Ozma. "I merely asked the magic belt to bring Dorothy and her party here to Oz."

"Glinda and Ozma," said Dorothy. "This is Dr. Rob Patterns, Professor of Music at the college I work for."

"Welcome, Dr. Rob Patterns," said Ozma. "Any friend of Dorothy is welcome in Oz. Glinda, what does your 'Book of Records' say about Dr. Rob Patterns?"

Glinda glanced at her book. "Oh you will be fine, Dr. Rob," said Glinda. "Here, why don't you read about it for yourself?"

"Well I, that is," began Dr. Rob. "I seem to have packed my reading glasses. They are in my luggage on the airplane."

"No problem!" replied Glinda. "I'll just have the book display the information in large print! Come. Have a look at it."

Dr. Rob walked over to the book and looked at it. He recognized his name and a few words here and there, but he really couldn't tell what the book said.

"Why yes!" replied Dr. Rob. "I see that I will land safely from that airplane ride."

"Really!" remarked Glinda. "The passage you were just looking at doesn't mention anything about your airplane ride. It talks about your safe arrival at Familyworld and your appearance at the Folk Music Center. You don't read very well do you?"

"All right," responded Dr. Rob. "I have a reading problem. In fact, I can't read much more than my own name." Dr. Rob looked at Dorothy, Katie and Tommy as if they had betrayed him.

"Don't look at us," said Dorothy. "We have kept your secret. You will find that it is very difficult to fool Glinda and Ozma. You gave yourself away."

"I'm sorry," said Dr. Rob. "I should be thanking you, not accusing you. Why do I have a feeling that all of this is going to work out for my good?"

"Well, this is the magical Land of Oz," said Dorothy. "Usually everything works out for the best in the end around here. I'm sorry you don't believe in the Land of Oz or helping you would be so much easier."

"I have heard about your stories about Oz, Dorothy," replied Dr. Rob. "But I didn't think they were true stories. I mean adults just don't believe such stories. So you really want me to believe that I am in the Land of Oz and that it is in the best interests for me."

"That's about the size of it Dr. Rob," said Dorothy.

"Dr. Rob," said Ozma. "I really should explain why you were invited to the Land of Oz. We have heard that you are good at interesting students in music. We would like you to help us set up a Music Department at the Athletic College of Oz. Oh, and we really did mean to bring you to Oz along with Dorothy, Katie and Tommy."

"And we knew about your reading problem, because we have been following Dorothy, Katie and Tommy on their trip to Familyland," added Glinda. "While you are helping us with establishing the Music department, I believe we can help you with your reading problem."

"I won't want to put you to any trouble," replied Dr. Rob. "But what am I to do about my engagement at the Folk Music center? I can't very well be at two places at once."

"If we promise that you will get to your engagement at the Folk Music center on time, would you be willing to help us?" asked Ozma.

"Well I do love music and teaching others to enjoy music," replied Dr. Rob. "If you will get me to the Folk Music center engagement as scheduled, then I am willing to help you with your Music Department."

"Fine!" replied Glinda and Ozma together. "We will get you to your engagement on time."

"So you brought Dr. Rob, Tommy, Katie and me to Oz to help you set up a Music Department for the Athletic College of Oz," said Dorothy. "I don't think Katie and Tommy really enjoy music lessons very much. How are they going to help with this project?"

"We noticed that Katie and Tommy found Dr. Rob's lesson on how to conduct music interesting at the airport this morning," said Ozma. "I feel that Dr. Rob can awaken their interest in music while he is here. But that isn't the only reason Tommy and Katie are here."

"Oh!" replied Katie and Tommy together. "Then why are we here?"

"Dorothy," said Glinda. "We know that you are supposed to help Katie and Tommy with their reading and spelling problems this summer. We thought we would give you some help in getting started on fixing their problems."

"That is very kind of you," replied Dorothy, Katie and Tommy, together.

"Mind you now," said Ozma. "Dr. Rob, Katie and Tommy will still have to do much work on their own if they are to overcome their problems. But we think we can help motivate you to want to solve your problems. We would also like to help you find the cause of your problem. If you know the cause of your problem, it will be easier to fix the problem."

"I think I have a spelling problem just because I am not as smart as the rest of the students in my class," said Tommy.

"And my reading problem comes from my being stupid," added Katie.

"I think I couldn't learn to read because of my being so interested in more abstract things such as music and art," added Dr. Rob.

"I am sure you can all be helped," said Glinda. "The first step is to admit that you have a problem. The second step is for you to want help. The three of you have already taken these two steps."

"Step three will be to discover the causes of your problems," added Ozma. "We will help you with that step. I believe that the Wizard and Professor Wogglebug can helps us out with this step. I'll have a messenger sent to the palace to tell the Wizard to meet us at the Athletic College of Oz, tomorrow afternoon. I will also request that the Sawhorse bring the carriage here by tomorrow morning. You can use it to travel to the college."

"You will be my guests for tonight," added Glinda. "In the morning, all of you can go on to the Athletic College of Oz.

My servants will show you to your quarters. Will you be so kind as to join me for dinner tonight?"

"Dinner with you sounds great!" replied Tommy.

Everyone else thought the idea was fine. So the servants showed Dorothy, Tommy, Katie and Dr. Rob to the guest quarters. They rested until dinner time. Then they joined Glinda for a small dinner in her quarters. The food, as it is always in Oz, was delicious.

Chapter 6 – Off to The College

The next morning, Dr. Rob, Tommy, Katie, Dorothy and Ozma, got up, got dressed and had breakfast in Ozma's guest quarters. They said farewell to Glinda and went out to the courtyard where the Sawhorse was waiting with the carriage. The Scarecrow of Oz had come along for the ride with the Sawhorse and was sitting in the front seat of the carriage.

"Either I need glasses, or there is a small wooden sawhorse, like a carpenter would use, hitched to that large carriage!" exclaimed Dr. Rob. "And look! The driver is a scarecrow! Is someone playing a joke on us?"

"That is the famous Wooden Sawhorse of Oz," said Katie.

"And you won't believe how fast he can pull that carriage," added Tommy.

"This is the magical kingdom of Oz," added Dorothy. "Trust us, that wooden sawhorse can pull that carriage much faster than you will want it to go."

"The driver of the carriage is the Scarecrow," added Tommy. "He is an ex-ruler of the Land of Oz and a friend of ours."

"He is alive and is very smart!" added Katie.

"Dr. Rob," said Ozma. "May I introduce the Wooden Sawhorse of Oz? Sawhorse, this is Dr. Rob a Professor of Music. He is going to set up a Music Department for the Athletic College of Oz."

"Hello," said Dr. Rob.

"Hello," responded the Sawhorse, much to Dr. Rob's surprise.

"He talks!" exclaimed Dr. Rob.

"And this is the Scarecrow," continued Ozma. "He is one of the wisest men in Oz. Scarecrow this is Dr. Rob, a friend of Dorothy."

"Any friend of Dorothy's is a friend of mine," replied the Scarecrow."

"Hi!" said Dr. Rob with some effort. He wasn't ready to believe his ears or eyes.

"That's all right," said the Scarecrow. "Adults have trouble believing in live scarecrows and sawhorses. It just takes time to get used to us."

"Come on. Let's all get aboard," suggested Dorothy.

So Dr. Rob, Ozma and Dorothy got in the back seat of the carriage. Tommy and Katie got into the front seat of the carriage on either side of the Scarecrow.

"Sawhorse!" said Ozma. "We would like to go to the Athletic College of Oz. We want to travel by way of China Country, Fuddlecumjig and Miss Cuttenclip."

"Is that all?" asked the Sawhorse.

"Well, we don't need to reach the college until dinnertime. So could you go slowly enough so that we can look at the scenery?" added Ozma.

"I knew it!" replied the Sawhorse. "You always want to go sightseeing."

"This is Dr. Rob's first visit to the Land of Oz," answered Ozma.

"It would help Dr. Rob believe in the Land of Oz if he gets to see some of the sights," added Dorothy.

"Well, for you, Ozma, I would do anything," replied the Sawhorse. He started pulling the carriage out of the courtyard of Glanda's Palace. Then he turned onto the road that led to China Country.

Dr. Rob was surprised at how easily the Sawhorse pulled the carriage. Even the Sawhorse's slow rate of travel seemed to be making good progress at covering the ground. The scenery still seemed to go by almost too fast to be seen.

This was Dr. Rob's first view of the Land of Oz. Since Glinda's palace was located at the far edge of Quadling Country, the trees and grass had a red hue.

"Why are the trees and grass red?" asked Dr. Rob.

"This is Quadling Country," answered Tommy. "It is one of the four countries in the Land of Oz."

"Its favorite color is red," continued Katie. "You may have noticed that the houses we passed are painted red and the people all dress in red outfits. Each country has its own color. That way, you know what country you are in."

"Well, I think one can over-do the use of a favorite color," replied Dr. Rob. "This sure isn't like any country I have ever seen before. Your Sawhorse does seem to handle this carriage well. If this is his slow speed, I am glad we are not in a hurry. So where is this college located where I am to set up the Music Department?"

"The Athletic College of Oz is located just inside of Munchkin Country," replied Ozma. "You will know when we cross into Munchkin Country by the way the color blue is favored. The Athletic College of Oz is also known as the Royal College of Oz. As you will find out, it is a most unusual college. Professor Wogglebug is the Dean of the college. He will help you set up the Music Department."

"Why do you want a Music Department at the college?" asked Dorothy. "I thought all the people of Oz already know how to sing just from the joy of being alive."

"Well, they do," replied Ozma. "But most of them don't know how to play any musical instruments. They have also expressed an interest in learning to do organized singing such as a barber shop quartet or a beauty shop quintet."

"There isn't a piano player in the whole Land of Oz," continued Ozma. "The musicians of the Royal Court Band and the Imperial Cornet Band of Oz are getting well up in age. Some of them want to retire. We need to train replacement players. Why the Land of Oz really needs to work on its music and dance abilities. We are a happy fairyland. There should be more music, singing and dancing."

"You don't have any organized music programs in the Land of Oz?" asked Dr. Rob.

"No, we don't," replied Ozma. "Oh, we do have a few people who seem to have natural talent for singing and dancing. But there has been no attempt at cultivating these talents. People just sing and dance anyway they feel like here in the Land of Oz."

"So parents don't have their children take music lessons here in the Land of Oz," added Dr. Rob. "And you only have a few bands and no orchestras?"

"That's right," replied Ozma. "We need someone to interest some of our citizens in learning to play musical instruments. Then we need people to teach others how to play the instruments. We also need to organize our singing and dancing."

"For starters," summed up Dr. Rob, "we need to train music teachers, directors and conductors. Each of them needs to know how to play several instruments. And above all else, they need to enjoy playing and teaching others about music."

"That sounds about right," said Dorothy. "Dr. Rob, do you think you can help us?"

"Well, I do have some good qualifications for the job," replied Dr. Rob. "For one thing, I like playing and teaching people about music. And I play several musical instruments."

"And he made it fun for Katie and me to learn how to conduct music," added Tommy.

"Maybe Dr. Rob can give us another music conducting lesson while we are here in Oz?" asked Katie.

"I think that can be arranged," replied Dr. Rob. "You two can join in with our first music class at the Athletic College of Oz. It will cover the basics of conducting or leading music."

They continued the discussion of what would be in the new Music Department for over an hour. Everyone had good suggestions for Dr. Rob. Soon, everyone lost track of where they were.

"Ozma," said Dorothy. "Do you know where we are?"

"I'm not sure," replied Ozma. "Has anyone seen a road sign recently?"

"I think I see a sign at the crossroad just up ahead," replied the Scarecrow.

"Sawhorse!" said Ozma. "Would you mind stopping at the crossroad up ahead so we can read what the sign says?"

"I'd be glad to," replied the Sawhorse.

The Sawhorse pulled up and stopped the carriage at the road sign.

The Scarecrow read the sign out loud. It said, "China Country, 0.5 mi." The sign pointed to the road on the right.

"Ozma?" asked Dorothy. "Can we show Dr. Rob China Country?"

"I don't see why not," replied Ozma. "Sawhorse, would you please turn right and take us to China Country?"

"As you command," replied the Sawhorse. He then took the road on the right and headed for China Country. Within a few minutes, the Sawhorse pulled up and stopped the carriage at the entrance to China Country.

"Is China Country part of the Land of Oz?" asked Dr. Rob.

"Oh yes!" replied Dorothy.

"What would a China Country have in it, in the Land of Oz?" asked Dr. Rob. "No! Don't tell me. Let me guess. China Country is a section of the Land of Oz where Oz craftsmen make fine china and figurines."

"Well, you are close, Dr. Rob," answered Dorothy. "But this isn't where they make the china figurines. It is where the china figurines live!"

"Oh my!" replied Dr. Rob. "First it was a live Sawhorse, then a live Scarecrow, and now it is live china figurines. What will I get to see next?"

Chapter 7 – China Country

China Country was surrounded by a high china wall. At the entrance, there was a door in the wall, with a door bell on it. A note had been attached to the door bell. The Scarecrow read it out loud, "Please don't bother us. We are brittle and strangers tend to break us!"

"Well, I see they still don't enjoy having visitors," said Tommy.

"You can't blame them," added Katie. "How would you like to be afraid that you might be broken at any time?"

"Perhaps we should leave them alone," suggested Dr. Rob. "I wouldn't want to cause any problems while I am in Oz."

"That's okay, Dr. Rob," said Ozma. "I am sure the Princess of China Country would like a visit with two former rulers of Oz and Princess Dorothy of Oz. Scarecrow, perhaps you could ring the bell for us?"

"I would be happy to," replied the Scarecrow. So he got down from the carriage and rang the door bell.

A couple of moments later a man made of china opened the door. He was about a foot tall. "Can't you read?" said the man. "Go away! We don't like visitors."

"Would you consider making an exception for two former rulers of Oz and Princess Dorothy of Oz?" asked the Scarecrow.

"Did you say two former rulers of Oz?" replied the man.

"Their Majesties, Ozma of Oz and the Scarecrow of Oz, would like to visit with Her Highness, the Princess of China Country," replied the Scarecrow. "Dorothy and her party would also like to be included."

"Yes, I am sure the Princess would like to have a visit with the former rulers of Oz," said the man. "Please have your party come on in. You can wait here on the pathway. I won't be long. But, please don't get off the path. Remember, we are brittle!"

So Ozma, Dorothy, Dr. Rob, Katie and Tommy got down from the carriage and entered China Country. The Sawhorse requested that he be allowed to stay outside. He had seen China Country once and had no wish to see it again.

Dorothy and the others began walking down the path that would take them to the Princess's palace. The inhabitants of China Country watched the visitors from a safe distance.

There were china butterflies flying overhead. The grass was made of china. The flowers were china. The houses were china. Everywhere the group looked, they saw things made out of china,

"You know, Dorothy," began the Scarecrow, "I haven't been to China Country since your

34

first visit to the Land of Oz. I wonder if that clown, Mr. Joker is still here."

"Well, he was still here on our trip with Joshua the ghost, to Oz," replied Dorothy. "At that time, Mr. Joker was still trying to learn to stand on his head."

The party followed the path around a curve that went between china trees which were full of singing china birds. Dr. Rob, Dorothy and the others were so intent at listening to the birds that they didn't watch where they were going. They had wondered off the path.

Just then, Mr. Joker the clown came by turning cart wheels and then trying to come to a stop in a headstand. He overshot the headstand and went flying into the Scarecrow, knocking them both to the ground. Fortunately, Mr. Joker landing on top of the Scarecrow and did not break anything. The Scarecrow, who was stuffed with straw, was also unhurt.

"You were fortunate that you ran into me," said the Scarecrow. "Or should we call it a lucky un-break for you, Mr. Joker? I was just wondering if you were still around."

"Yes!" replied Mr. Joker. "I was very fortunate to run into a person stuffed with straw. Otherwise, that fall could have sent me to the mending shop once again."

"Well, it has been many years since I last saw you," continued the Scarecrow. "But I believe you have been mended many times since our last meeting."

"You know, Mr. Joker," said Dorothy. "There really must be a better way for you to practice standing on your head. I know you are made out of china. But even so it should be possible for you to do acrobatics without fear of needing mending. What do you think, Scarecrow?"

"I think if Mr. Joker would get up off of me, then I could think better," replied the Scarecrow. "It is difficult for me to think with a clown on my stomach."

"I am so sorry," replied Mr. Joker. "Please forgive me." Mr. Joker got to his feet and bowed to Ozma and Dorothy.

"What a pleasure to see you once more," said Mr. Joker.

"Mr. Joker," said Dorothy. "This is Dr. Rob. This is his first visit to the Land of Oz. I am sure Dr. Rob has never seen a live china clown before."

"Dr. Rob," continued Dorothy. "This is Mr. Joker the clown. He is an old friend of mine. He is willing to try doing what most people consider to be impossible."

"Hello, Mr. Joker," replied Dr. Rob. "I am glad to meet you."

"Hello," replied Mr. Joker, and then he broke into a rhyme.

"It is my pleasure,
As you can see
For me to meet
Friends of Dorothy.

And how fortunate of all
For me to renew
An acquaintance with
My old friend the Scarecrow!" continued Mr. Joker.

"You know," said the Scarecrow, who had now regained his feet. "I have been thinking about your problem of always getting broken."

"Oh!" replied Mr. Joker, with surprise. "Don't tell me that you think I should give up trying to stand on my head?"

"Oh no!" replied the Scarecrow. "I won't discourage anyone from trying to do something new. No indeed! What I had in mind is a safer way for you to do practice standing on your head."

"Well, I guess you could just follow me around and make sure you get under me whenever I start to fall," suggested Mr. Joker.

"Now that's not a bad idea," added Tommy.

"True," said the Scarecrow. "However, I think I have an even better idea. Why don't we build you a big practice area that is covered with thick straw? That way if you fall, the straw would protect you from being broken."

"Now why didn't I think of that?" asked Mr. Joker. "That is a very good idea!"

"Perhaps you didn't think of it because you are made of china," suggested Tommy.

"So you would have had them make the straw practice area out of china," added Katie. "Then you would have broken the china straw as well as yourself!"

"I think we should also get a circus clown to come and teach Mr. Joker how to stand on his head," added Tommy.

Just then the china man door keeper returned.

"I beg your pardon," said the china man door keeper. "I believe I asked you to stay on the path!"

"I am sorry!" replied Ozma. "We seemed to have gotten distracted by the singing of the china birds. We will get right back on the path."

"See that you do!" replied the door keeper. "Her Highness, the Princess of China Country would like to talk with you. Now if you will please follow me."

So everyone followed the door keeper back to the path and on to the palace of the Princess of China country. The Princess and Her court came out to greet Ozma, the Scarecrow, Dorothy and friends.

"Your Majesties, Highness, and friends," said the Princess of China Country. "Welcome to China Country. What can we do for you?"

"We were in the neighborhood and wanted to show Dr. Rob around China Country," replied Ozma. "This is Dr. Rob's first visit to the Land of Oz. He is here to help set up a Music Department for the Athletic College of Oz."

"Welcome to China Country, Dr. Rob," said the Princess of China Country. "Any friend of Ozma, the Scarecrow, and Dorothy is welcome here. Did you say you are setting up a music department at the Athletic College of Oz?"

"Yes, we are," replied Ozma.

"Do you think you might have the music department visit us?" asked the China Princess.

"I believe that can be arranged," agreed Ozma.

"Please allow us to give you a short tour of China Country," continued the China Princess.

So Ozma, the Scarecrow, Dorothy, and the others followed Her Highness, the Princess of China Country on a short tour. Mr. Joker joined them. He told Her Highness about the Scarecrow's suggestion for a real straw practice area. Her Highness liked the idea.

When the tour was over, Ozma promised the Princess of China Country that she would send straw and workmen to put in the practice area. When the area is ready for use, a circus clown will visit Mr. Joker. The music department will also plan a visit to China Country. Finally, everyone said their goodbyes. Ozma and her party then left China Country and got back into their carriage.

Chapter 8 -- Fuddlecumjig

"Sawhorse!" said Ozma. "May we continue on to the Athletic College of Oz?"

"Right away, Your Majesty," replied the Sawhorse. He then turned the carriage around and headed back for the main road. Upon reaching the main road, he turned right and continued pulling the carriage towards the Athletic College of Oz.

"Dr. Rob," said Dorothy. "Do you believe that you are in the Land of Oz yet?"

"Well, I don't know about being in the Land of Oz," replied Dr. Rob. "But I am sure I have never heard of live china figurines in the non-magical outside world. Therefore, I must not be in the outside world. So this must be some kind of magic or fairyland."

"The Land of Oz is a magic fairyland," said Tommy. "You know, for an adult, you are taking all of this very well."

"Tommy is right!" added Katie. "You should hear how our mother reacted to being brought to the Land of Oz. She simply refused to believe that it happened. It took several days to convince her that she was in Oz."

"Right!" added Dorothy. "Your mother met the Wizard, the Scarecrow, the Tin Woodman, and the Cowardly Lion. And yet she still thought it was just a bad dream."

"I will try to believe what I see and hear," replied Dr. Rob. "Since living china is not part of the outside world, I find it easier to believe I am in the magic Land of Oz. It is easier than trying to explain how these things could be happening. The Sawhorse and the Scarecrow are also convincing proof of this being some special land!"

"Well, I like how easily you adjust to our Land of Oz," said Ozma. "I am glad that you seem to be enjoying yourself."

"Have you given any thought to what musical instruments you will need for your work at the college?" continued Ozma. "I believe you like the piano and banjo. So I have make arrangements for several pianos and banjos to be waiting for us at the college."

"Yes I do like the piano and banjo," replied Dr. Rob. "Thank you for getting some for me. However I hadn't thought about other musical instruments yet. I will need a pitch-pipe, some sheet music, some recorded music, and I can only begin to guess at what other instruments I will need. Let me think about this question for a while."

"Perhaps you will need some books on music appreciation?" suggested Tommy.

"Or maybe some books on the history of music," suggested Katie.

"But I can't read those books!" answered Dr. Rob. "What will my students think about me when they find out that they can read the books and their teacher can't?"

"Well, I can't help you out with that problem," replied Ozma. "But I can give you a temporary fix to your problem that will only work while we are on our way to the Athletic College of Oz!"

"What?" replied Tommy, Katie and Dr. Rob together.

"Why I am going to let Dr. Rob find out what it is like to be able to read," answered Ozma, as she waved her magic wand at Dr. Rob. "Now about what musical instruments and other things you will want for the Music Department of the college."

So the group discussed what it would be nice to have in the way of materials and equipment for the Music Department. The discussion lasted for over an hour. Once more, the group lost track of where they were.

The grass and trees still had a red hue, so they were still somewhere in Quadling Country. Fortunately, they were just approaching a crossroads.

"Sawhorse," requested Ozma, "would you mind stopping at the road sign at that crossroads just ahead?"

"As you wish, Ozma," replied the Sawhorse. "You know I would do anything for you." So the Sawhorse pulled the carriage up to the road sign and stopped.

"Dr. Rob," said Ozma. "Have you ever had trouble finding your way around because you can't read the road signs?"

"Well, yes I have," replied Dr. Rob. "While I do know a few names, but it usually isn't enough for me to find my way around in a strange neighborhood. It is one reason for my wishing I could learn to read."

"Well, for the rest of this trip," started Ozma, "you will be able to read! Okay?"

"Wow!" replied Dr. Rob. "I don't believe it! Well that is, I do believe it, but I didn't think that I would ever get to experience reading. When do I get to start reading?"

"Why don't you start by reading that road sign?" suggested Dorothy.

"Okay!" replied Dr. Rob. "Here I go! The sign says 'This Way To Fuddlecumjig' and has an arrow pointing to the right. Wow! I can read!"

"Very good, Dr. Rob," replied Ozma. "I want you to enjoy being able to read, but remember that this is only temporary!"

"I will enjoy it and I will remember that it is temporary," replied Dr. Rob. "Thank you for this present! Now I believe that I am in the magical Land of Oz."

"What's Fuddlecumjig?" asked Katie.

"How far is it and do they serve lunch?" asked Tommy.

"It is far easier to let you experience Fuddlecumjig than to describe it to you," replied Dorothy. "I haven't been to Fuddlecumjig since my fifth trip to Oz oh so many years ago. However, Fuddlecumjig is where the Fuddles live."

"Well I think we should visit Fuddlecumjig," said Ozma. "Sawhorse, would you mind turning for Fuddlecumjig?"

"Right away, Your Majesty," replied the Sawhorse. He then took the road on the right and headed for Fuddlecumjig.

"Oh and Tommy," added Ozma. "Fuddlecumjig is about a mile from here. And yes, we can get some lunch there."

"In that case," said Tommy, "what are we waiting for? Can't the Sawhorse go faster?"

"Well, yes the Sawhorse can go faster, Tommy, but I don't recommend it," said Dorothy.

"Why?" asked Katie.

"Well, we don't want to make the citizens of Fuddlecumjig nervous," replied Dorothy. "If you will look closely at some of the people working in the fields, you will see that some of them are starting to fall apart from just seeing us headed for Fuddlecumjig."

"Oh dear!" replied Katie. "What kind of place is this?"

"Did the Nome King have them cubed or something?" asked Tommy.

"These people are citizens of Fuddlecumjig," replied Ozma. "They are living jig-saw puzzles. Unfortunately, when strangers come by, these citizens tend to come all apart. Then the strangers will have to reassemble them before they can meet these citizens."

"I thought jig-saw puzzles were flat?" said Tommy.

"Well, in the last few years, they have also been making three-dimensional jig-saw puzzles," answered Katie. "Of course those three-dimensional jig-saw puzzles aren't alive."

"Perhaps not," agreed Dorothy. "However, the outside non-magical world might have gotten their idea for three-dimensional jig-saw puzzles from stories about Oz."

About this time, the Sawhorse stopped the carriage in front of a small village. The group climbed down from the carriage and headed for a big building. This was the town hall of Fuddlecumjig. As they approached the building Dorothy saw the mayor. He immediately fell apart. Dorothy and Scarecrow quickly reassembled him.

The mayor invited them to lunch. They walked inside. Here they found several persons in pieces.

"I thought we were here to have lunch?" said Tommy. He didn't seem to think having to reassemble Fuddles was a substitute for eating.

"Oh we are!" replied Ozma. "However, first we need to reassemble our hosts before they can cook us lunch."

"So let me see if I understand everything," said Dr. Rob. "We have here living three-dimension jig-saw puzzles that we need to put together before they can invite us to lunch. And if we don't get them reassemble, what will happen?"

"Why we will get very hungry," said Tommy.

"Don't worry about Tommy," said Katie. "He is always hungry. I don't think missing a meal would do him any real harm."

"Maybe not," said Dorothy. "But we wouldn't want Tommy to go hungry unnecessarily. Let's start by putting together the Fuddles in here."

"How do you do that?" asked Dr. Rob. "I mean which parts belong to which Fuddle? It is harder to solve three puzzles that have all their pieces mixed together."

"Well, we may need the help of the Fuddles," said Dorothy. "If we can just find eyes and mouths and maybe some noses, we should be able to get the Fuddles help." So everyone looked around for pieces that contained mouths, eyes, and noses.

Soon the group had found enough pieces to include five eyes, two mouths and three noses. Next they tried to arrange the pieces so that they began to make three faces. With much effort, they managed to get the three faces almost together.

The Fuddles responded by all talking at once. They were trying very hard to help Dorothy and her party to reassemble them. But no one could understand what was being said.

"What do we do now?" shouted Dr. Rob. "I can't make out what they are saying."

"We need to find some ears," shouted Dorothy. "Then we can get them to talk one at a time." So everyone looked around the room for pieces that contained ears. It took several minutes before they were able to come up with five ears. Once these were attached to the right heads, the three Fuddles become more orderly.

"I'M THE COOK".

"Now then," started Dorothy, "we want all three of you Fuddles to be quiet and listen. We are going to reassemble you one at a time. Let's start with the Fuddle on my right."

So with the aid of the first Fuddle, the group finished assembling its head and began to gather together the pieces making up its body. It turned out to be a lady Fuddle. She

43

was just about ready to start cooking lunch. While the lady Fuddle cooked the lunch, Dorothy, the Scarecrow, Tommy, Katie, and Dr. Rob finished assembling the other two Fuddles.

The group was getting so good at the puzzles that they then went out in the street and assembled three more Fuddles before lunch was ready. The mayor and the six other Fuddles sat down and eat lunch with Dorothy and her party.

"I am curious!" said Dr. Rob to the lady Fuddle. "Why do you come all apart when strangers come by?"

"Well, didn't you find putting us back together interesting and entertaining?" asked the lady Fuddle.

"Yes I did!" replied Dr. Rob. "What about you Tommy and Katie?"

"Well that was sure a different experience," agreed Tommy. "I guess I did enjoy the challenge."

"It was much more fun than just working two-dimensional jig-saw puzzles," added Katie.

"So you see we just fall all apart to entertain our visitors," replied the lady Fuddle. "Entertaining visitors is always challenging. I am glad you enjoyed yourselves."

So Dorothy, Katie, Tommy, Dr. Rob and Ozma had lunch with the Fuddles. The main course was Quadling Stew. There was red bread, red milk and many red vegetables. As they ate, they talked with the Fuddles.

"Tell me, Dr. Rob, why are you visiting Oz?" asked the lady Fuddle.

"I am here to organize a music department for the Athletic college of Oz," replied Dr. Rob.

"You mean you will teach people to play musical instruments?" suggested the lady Fuddle.

"Yes, it will include that along with singing and teaching people to teach others about music," responded Dr. Rob.

"I hope we can participate in the music program," stated the lady Fuddle.

"I will arrange it so you can do that," promised Ozma.

While the others were eating lunch, the Scarecrow went out and reassembled more of the Fuddles. He was so intent on his work, that before he knew it, the others had finished lunch and had joined him in the task of putting the Fuddles together again.

The group soon had the task completed. Finally, they said goodbye to the Fuddles and got back on the carriage.

"Sawhorse," said Ozma, "we wish to continue on our way to the Athletic College of Oz."

"As you wish," replied the Sawhorse. He then turned the carriage around and headed for the main road.

Chapter 9 – Miss Cuttenclip

The Sawhorse turned right at the main road and continued the journey to the college. Dorothy and the others were full from just having enjoyed a good lunch and didn't feel much like talking. So the group traveled along in silence for some time.

The scenery rolled along for over an hour when Tommy finally asked, "Where are we?"

"Well, I don't know," replied Dorothy. "Has anyone seen a road sign recently?"

"No!" replied everyone.

"Wait a minute," said Dr. Rob. "I think I see a road side just up ahead!"

"Sawhorse," commanded Ozma. "Would you mind stopping at that road side just up ahead?"

"As you wish!" replied the Sawhorse. He then pulled the carriage up to the road sign and stopped.

"Dr. Rob!" asked Ozma. "Would you be so kind as to read the road sign for us?"

"I will do so happily," replied Dr. Rob. "The sign says, 'Take This Road To The Cuttenclips.' Does that mean anything to any of you?"

"We have never been to Cuttenclips," replied Tommy and Katie together.

"Well, I was there on my fifth visit to Oz," replied Dorothy. "And of course Ozma knows about the Cuttenclips."

"I remember the road to the Cuttenclips as not being very good," added the Sawhorse. "Don't tell me you want to visit there again."

"If we are near the Cuttenclips," said Ozma, "then we are almost to the Athletic College of Oz. It is still early in the afternoon, and Professor Wogglebug isn't expecting us until dinnertime. I think we should visit the Cuttenclips so Dr. Rob, Tommy and Katie can see the Cuttenclips."

"Okay!" replied the Sawhorse as he turned the carriage in the direction for the Cuttenclips. "And you won't have to ask me to go slowly, this time. The road isn't all that good and this is a large carriage."

The road got rougher and the houses became fewer as the carriage progressed on its way to the Cuttenclips. However, the magical Sawhorse was soon able to stop the carriage in front of a high circular blue wall with pink ornaments. The wall enclosed a large area. There was a path leading to a small door in the wall, which was closed and latched. Next to the door was a sign with gold lettering.

"Dr. Rob?" asked Ozma. "Would you mind reading the sign for us?"

"But of course!" replied Dr. Rob, who was enjoying being able to read. "It says, 'Visitors are requested to Move Slowly and Carefully, and to avoid Coughing or making any Breeze or Draft.' Wow, the Cuttenclips sure sound like strange people."

46

"Well, they are a little unusual," replied Dorothy. "Before we visit the Cuttenclips, we need to set some ground rules. First, if anyone has allergies or a cold, they should wait out here. Second, we are all to stay together on the path and don't laugh or even talk loud. And, third, we all move very slowly and carefully!"

"Okay, I agree to the rules," said Tommy. "But why do we need all the rules?"

"Why because the Cuttenclips are paper dolls and can easily be damaged!" replied Ozma.

"The last time I visited here the Shaggyman was with me. He sneezed and blow over a large part of their town," recalled Dorothy. "These paper dolls blow over easily."

"Oh goodie!" exclaimed Katie. "I always liked paper dolls. But I don't know if Tommy and Dr. Rob will enjoy this visit."

"Oh I don't know," answered Tommy. "So far every place we visited in the Land of Oz has been very interesting. I am sure there must be something special about these paper dolls."

"Tommy is right!" said Ozma. "These paper dolls are made from magic paper that allows them to come alive! I am sure that Tommy and Dr. Rob will find this visit very interesting."

"That reminds me," continued Ozma. "I have some more magic paper, from Glinda, in the back of the carriage. We can deliver the paper while we are here."

So the group walked up the path to the door. The Scarecrow led the way and opened the door very slowly for the others. As soon as the group was inside, the Scarecrow closed the door. A line of paper soldiers with paper guns surrounded the group.

"Hello there," said the Captain of the soldiers. "May we help you?"

"Why yes!" replied Ozma. "Would you please tell Miss Cuttenclip that Ozma is here for a visit with some friends? Also tell her that I have some more magic paper for her."

"Wow!" shouted Tommy. "Those paper soldiers look so real!"

Of course the breeze from Tommy's shout knocked over the Captain. The Captain landed flat on his back.

"Do be more careful!" said the Captain.

"I am sorry," whispered Tommy, and then he offered his hand to the Captain. The Captain accepted his hand and was lifted back onto his feet.

"You must speak more softly, or you will blow over the whole town," said the Captain. "Now if you will just follow me, I will take you to Miss Cuttenclip."

"These Cuttenclips seem to be very delicate!" added Katie in a soft voice.

"Actually, we are strong and healthy," replied the Captain. "But we can't stand up to drafts. Please go slowly and speak very softly as we go through the town. Remember, everything you see is made out of paper."

So Dorothy and her friends followed the Captain very carefully. They saw rows of paper trees and cardboard houses. There was a cardboard school with paper school children out at recess. All the paper people were wearing very bright outfits. There were paper flower gardens with beautiful flowers in bloom. Paper dogs chased paper cats. Many paper people were walking about on the paper streets. In the center of the town, there were cardboard shops of all types. There was also a cardboard church and city hall.

When the paper people saw the strangers coming, they ran back into to their homes, businesses, or school. They peeked out of the windows at the strangers. By the time the group reached the center of the town, the streets were deserted.

"We seem to be scaring the Cuttenclips," said Dr. Rob.

"No, you are not," replied the Captain. "It is just so unnerving to be knocked over by a slight breeze. We are really happy to see strangers. But we have also learned to use caution."

"We will turn right here," continued the Captain. "Miss Cuttenclip's house is up on that hill."

Tommy, Katie and the others looked up the hill pointed out to them by the Captain. They saw a small house on the hill, made for an ordinary person. The house looked huge next to the cardboard town.

It took them several minutes to walk up the hill to the house. The Captain entered the house and announced the arrival of Ozma, Dorothy and the others. Miss Cuttenclip invited them all to come inside. She was a small girl about seven years old. In the living room, Miss Cuttenclip was working on cutting out more paper dolls.

"Won't you sit down?" asked Miss Cuttenclip as she cleared paper scraps off of the chairs and sofa. "I don't get visitors very often. This is my workshop and it is pretty untidy."

Introductions were made all around.

"What brings you to Cuttenclip?" asked Miss Cuttenclip.

"We are taking Dr. Rob to the Athletic College of Oz to start a new music department," replied Ozma.

"I wonder if my dolls would be interested in playing music?" said Miss Cuttenclip. "I am sure that they would enjoy hearing some music!"

"You and some of your dolls will have to visit the college after the music program gets under way," replied Ozma. "We will let you know when a performance is going to take place."

Dr. Rob looked around the room. On one table were paints and brushes, along with scissors of all sizes. He asked, "Did you make all the houses, trees, and paper people?"

"Why yes I did," replied Miss Cuttenclip. "I am the queen here and made everything you saw."

"The paper that Ozma has for you looks just like most paper," said Tommy. "How do you bring the paper dolls made from it to life?"

"The paper from Glinda the Good is magical!" replied Miss Cuttenclip. "Once I have finished cutting the doll out and decorated it, I just set it upright and it just comes to life all by itself. I then give it a name and find it a place in my village."

"Please come with me and I will show you all my many years of work," invited Miss Cuttenclip.

"Many years of work?" questioned Katie. "But Miss Cuttenclip, you don't look any older than I am."

"You must remember that people don't age here in the Land of Oz," replied Miss Cuttenclip. "Your Auntie Dorothy spent many years here in Oz. Does she look like she is one hundred years old?"

"Well, no she doesn't," answered Tommy.

"Well, she made her first visit to the Land of Oz in 1900. Dorothy was only seven years old at that time."

"You mean Dorothy was born around 1890," asked Dr. Rob. "That is amazing! She only looks about fifty!"

"Well, thanks a lot," replied Dorothy. "I always like to think of myself as looking younger than I am!"

50

Miss Cuttenclip showed the group all around her town. She also showed the group her work on a new farm just outside of the town. Miss Cuttenclip was very proud of her paper farm animals.

After the tour, Miss Cuttenclip escorted the group back to the door in the wall.

"Thank you for showing all of us around your town and farm," said Dorothy. "I know we all enjoyed the tour."

"You're quite welcome," replied Miss Cuttenclip. "I enjoyed showing you around. Please drop by again sometime."

The group said good bye and got back into the carriage. Now everyone was able to take deep breaths and talk loudly.

"Sawhorse," said Ozma. "Would you take us to the Athletic College of Oz?"

"Right away!" replied the Sawhorse and started once more for the college.

Chapter 10 -- The Athletic College of Oz

Since no one seemed to care how fast the Sawhorse was going, he decided to travel a little faster than before. Within the hour, the group noticed that the scenery had changed. The grass and trees no longer came in a red hue. Instead, the grass and trees had a blue hue.

"Why have the trees and grass changed to a blue hue?" asked Dr. Rob.

"Because we have crossed into Munchkin Country," replied Tommy.

"Here in Munchkin Country, the favorite color is blue," added Katie. "We must be almost to the Athletic College."

"It should be about fifteen more minutes at this rate of travel," said Dorothy. "It will be nice to see Professor Wogglebug once more."

Within ten minutes, they arrived at the Athletic College of Oz. The Sawhorse pulled the carriage onto the college grounds and stopped by the athletic fields. Here Professor Wogglebug was busy watching his students practice their athletic skills.

Ozma, Dorothy, Katie, Tommy, the Scarecrow and Dr. Rob got down from the carriage. They walked over to where Professor Wogglebug was standing.

"Excuse me, Professor Wogglebug," said Ozma. "I would like to introduce you to Dr. Rob, a Professor of Music, my Niece Katie and Nephew Tommy."

Professor Wogglebug turned around. It was then that Dr. Rob, Katie and Tommy got their first good look at him.

"Oh my goodness!" exclaimed Dr. Rob. "You're a big bug! In fact you are the biggest bug I have ever seen!"

Tommy and Katie were also surprised by the Professor's appearance.

Finally, Tommy said, "Of course he is a bug, Dr. Rob. That is why we call him Professor Wogglebug."

"If he is a friend of Ozma's then he must be a very friendly bug," added Katie. "And of course he is the most intelligent bug a person could ever meet!"

"We, I . . . That is," stuttered Dr. Rob. "I am sure glad to hear that you are a friendly bug. How do you do?"

"I am very fine," replied Professor Wogglebug. "I am Dean of the Royal College of Oz. It is better known as the

Athletic College of Oz. Did Ozma say you are a Professor of Music?"

"Yes, Ozma said I am a Professor of Music," replied Dr. Rob. "I believe I am here to help you start a Music Department."

"Yes you are," replied Professor Wogglebug. "We want to add music training to our curriculum. It is one area in which we don't have any courses at present."

"I see you have a number of athletic teams," remarked Dr. Rob. "Is there some competition going on or are all these students from your college?"

"These are all students from our college," replied Professor Wogglebug. "They spend many hours a day practicing their athletic skills. It is a physical skill. One requires many hours of practice before one becomes proficient at it."

"What about the usual courses in reading, writing and arithmetic?" asked Dr. Rob. "Surely they also require many hours of practice?"

"Well, we have Education Pills for learning the mental skills needed for reading, writing, arithmetic, history, science, and so forth," replied Professor Wogglebug. "Of course there are some physical skills required in reading and writing. These do require practicing."

"Most of playing music is a mechanical skill," stated Dr. Rob. "If you have a Music Department, your students will need to practice their music playing at least an hour a day!"

"That's why we need help in starting a Music Department," replied Professor Wogglebug. "I can come up with a music pill for learning about the history and fundamentals of music, but I don't have the physical skills developed for playing music."

"Okay then, when do I start working on the Music Department?" asked Dr. Rob.

"Well, now it is almost time for dinner," answered Professor Wogglebug. "I think all of you should get settled in our guest professor quarters. After that, we will all get together for dinner at the college dining hall. Most of your work on the Music Department won't be started before tomorrow."

"Actually the Sawhorse and I are not staying," replied Ozma. "I have other duties to take care of. I am sure the Scarecrow, Dorothy and the others can take care of any questions you might have. I'll say good bye for now."

So everyone said good bye to Ozma and the Sawhorse. Ozma got into the carriage and had the Sawhorse pull it back to the Emerald City.

Dorothy, Katie, Tommy, the Scarecrow and Dr. Rob were shown to the guest professors' quarters. They rested for a while and then got ready for dinner.

Dorothy and her friends gathered together in the hallway of the guest quarters. A student then took them over to the college dining hall.

Another student showed them the way to the table where Professor Wogglebug was sitting with another person. That person was the Wizard of Oz. They stood up as Dorothy and her party approached the table.

"Hello Wizard and Professor Wogglebug," said Dorothy as she and the others sat down. "Wizard, I would like you to meet Dr. Rob, Professor of Music. Dr. Rob, this is the Wizard of Oz. The Wizard was the ruler of the Land of Oz when I first visited Oz."

"Hello, it's nice to meet you!" said the Wizard and Dr. Rob to each other.

"What kind of Wizard are you?" asked Dr. Rob.

"Why I am a good wizard and getting better all the time," replied the Wizard. The Wizard placed his hat on the table in front of himself. He said a few magic words that no one could quite understand and then proceeded to pull the Scarecrow out of his hat. This surprised everyone at the table including the Scarecrow.

"I wish you would warn me before you do that!" exclaimed the Scarecrow. "That trick almost took my breath away."

"Well, it might take your breath away if you actually could breathe," added Dorothy.

"But how did you do that?" asked Dr. Rob.

"I am sorry," replied the Wizard. "I am not allowed to give away trade secrets."

"Scarecrow?" asked Dr. Rob. "How did he do that to you? You were right behind me just before the Wizard did that trick."

"I am not sure," replied the Scarecrow. "One minute, I was right behind you and the next minute I found myself coming out of the Wizard's hat. Now that trick gave me a very strange feeling."

"You are right, Scarecrow," said the Wizard. "I should have warned you before I used you in a trick. You have my apologies."

"Why are you here?" asked Dorothy. "Are you going to help Dr. Rob with setting up the Music Department?"

"I am sure that I will help Dr. Rob and Professor Wogglebug with setting up the Music department," replied the Wizard. "However, I am mainly here to help Katie, Tommy and Dr. Rob find the causes of their reading and spelling problems."

"Which of us are you going to help first?" asked Tommy.

"Well, I think I will start with Katie's problem," replied the Wizard. "I think she may have the easiest problem to solve. Of course Katie is a lady and ladies get helped first."

"Professor Wogglebug has also said that he would make available all the resources of the college to help solve your problems," continued the Wizard. "I think that I will wait until tomorrow morning to work on your problems. That way you will all be well rested."

"Dr. Rob," Professor Wogglebug suggested. "We can start getting students interested in the new music program this evening. We could have a sing-along after dinner. What do you think about that idea?"

"Well, I think a sing-along would be nice," replied Dr. Rob. "It is too bad that I didn't bring my banjo and piano with me."

"How large would your piano be?" asked the Wizard.

"Why it is just a baby grand piano," replied Dr. Rob. "It's about four feet high, eight feet wide, and eight feet deep.

The piano probably weighs around three hundred pounds. The banjo is much smaller. Its case is about one foot by three feet."

"Ozma had your piano and banjo delivered here last night," replied the Wizard. "She also delivered all of your luggage."

"That was very kind of her," replied Dr. Rob. "Where are my banjo and piano?"

"They are behind the curtain, up on that stage over there," pointed the Wizard. "You can check them out after you have finished eating."

"So are we going to have a sing-along after dinner?" asked Tommy and Katie, together.

"Unless someone had some objection, I believe we will have a sing-long once dinner is finished!" replied Dr. Rob. "Perhaps Professor Wogglebug could arrange an announcement to the students?"

Professor Wogglebug called a student over to him. He gave the student a message. Shortly thereafter, the public address system announced the forthcoming sing-along.

The rest of the dinner hour was taken up with small talk and eating a variety of foods. Finally, when they all thought they couldn't eat another bite, they had to choose between a wide selection of desserts.

After the dining was done, the students sat around in small groups waiting for the sing-along to start. Dr. Rob, the Wizard, the Scarecrow, Professor Wogglebug, Dorothy, Katie and Tommy went up to the stage. Here, Dr. Rob examined his piano and banjo. He also checked on what sheet music he had available.

Dr. Rob began tuning his banjo with the aid of the piano. He let Katie press the desired keys as he tuned the banjo.

After the banjo was tuned, Dr. Rob sat down at the piano and did some warm up exercises. Finally, he was ready to start the sing-along.

The sing-along started by having the group sing a verse of a song. Next the students joined in the second time around. This method was used to teach several round songs to the students.

Next, Professor Wogglebug, the Wizard and Dorothy led three groups of students in singing the round songs of: "Row, row, row your boat"; "A bicycle built for two"; and "Down at the station, early in the morning." Dr. Rob accompanied the singing using the piano.

After the students were worn out, Dr. Rob did a short concert using his banjo and finally his piano. Everyone enjoyed the sing-along.

When the sing-along ended, many students waited around to talk with Dr. Rob. Several students expressed an interest in learning how to play the banjo. More students expressed an interest in learning to play the piano. All these students wanted more information about the new music program for the college.

Professor Wogglebug took down notes on the students' names and interests. He assured everyone that they would receive more information on the music program, tomorrow afternoon.

It had been a long day for Dorothy and her friends, so it was decided that they should all go to bed and get a good night's sleep. Everyone said good night to everyone else and went to their quarters. Soon, all were fast asleep.

Chapter 11 – Having Fun Reading and Spelling

The next morning, Dorothy, Katie, Tommy, and Dr. Rob, got up, got dressed and went to Professor Wogglebug's quarters. They had breakfast with Professor Wogglebug, the Scarecrow and the Wizard. After the meal Professor Wogglebug announced what the activities were for the day.

"This morning, all of you will be looking over examination copies of possible books for the new music program," started Professor Wogglebug. "Tommy, you will act as the note taker and keep track of all the comments made by the other members of your team. You will need to use both pencil and paper and the chalk board."

"You know I have a spelling problem," replied Tommy. "Wouldn't it be better to have Auntie Dorothy take the notes?"

"Yes, I know you have trouble with spelling," replied Professor Wogglebug. "Ozma gave me permission to try out a new spelling pill on you. You will see it next to you water glass. Please take it now with some water. It will let you spell like a smart high school graduate for the rest of the morning!"

"Thank you, Professor," said Tommy. He picked up the pill and swallowed it with the aid of a sip of water.

"Professor Wogglebug," said Dr. Rob. "I am sure I can evaluate the musical instruments and sheet music. I can even suggest what courses should make up the curriculum. But I won't be able to evaluate the textbooks. This morning I found out that I can't read anymore."

"If you will look next to your water glass, Dr. Rob, you will see a new reading pill," stated the Professor. "It will allow you to read like a college graduate for this morning!"

"I don't like to take pills. But I'll gladly take this pill," said Dr. Rob, as he picked up and took the pill.

"I see there is a pill by my water glass too!" added Katie. "I guess if I swallow this pill then I can expect to be able to read college level textbooks!"

"You are correct!" replied Professor Wogglebug.

So Katie took her pill.

After breakfast, Professor Wogglebug took Dorothy, Tommy, Katie, Dr. Rob, the Wizard, and the Scarecrow to his office next to the dining hall. Here Katie and Tommy were able to see some of the bottles of learning pills.

Then they went to a nearby classroom. In the classroom were desks, chairs, several blackboards with chalk, erasers, pencils, pads of paper, stacks of books, stacks of sheet music, and many musical instruments.

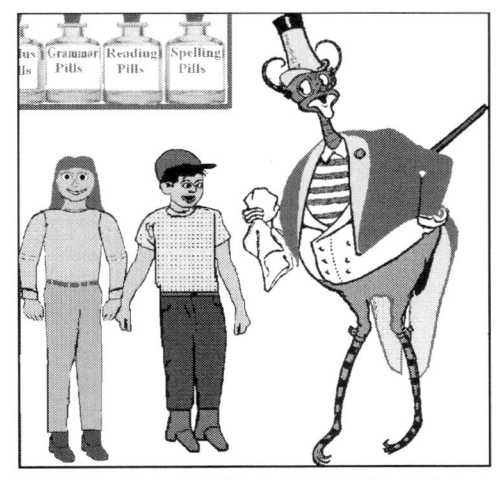

The Professor walked over to the first stack of books. "This stacks of books contains possible textbooks for an introductory music course," said Professor Wogglebug. "This next stack is for the history of music. Here we have several stacks on teaching music to different age groups."

The Professor continued in this fashion until he had accounted for all the stacks of books. Finally, he left the group to work on their own.

"Let's start with the introduction to music books," said Dr. Rob. "How many books are there in the stack?"

"I count ten books," said Tommy.

"Let's place one book on each desk in this row," suggested Katie.

"We can have Tommy put each of our names in a column on the backboard with the numbers one through ten across the board," added Dorothy.

"And each of us can then look at each book and rate them from one to ten, ten being the best," suggested the Scarecrow.

"But first we need to list what topics we need to cover in the course," said the Wizard. "Dr. Rob, what topics need to be covered in an introductory music course?"

"Well, we need to define what music is," began Dr. Rob. "Next we need a short and interesting history of music. Then we need . . ."

While Dr. Rob was talking, Tommy took notes on the blackboard. He was amazed at the words he could spell correctly.

"In conclusion," continued Dr. Rob, "if we just look at the table of contents of this first book, you will see it starts off

59

with what is music." Much to his surprise, he was actually reading the table of contents of the book. Dr. Rob was pleased to find that the table of contents closely followed the notes that Tommy had made on the blackboard.

"Why don't each of us take a pad of paper and then start by looking at this first book?" suggested Dorothy. "We should write down what we like and dislike about each book as we compare its contents to the first book."

Katie picked up a pencil and a pad of paper, and went over and looked at the first textbook. She was surprised to learn that she could read not only the table of contents, but the regular chapters as well. Reading had never been so easy or so much fun for her before.

Everyone proceeded to examine the first textbook on introduction to music. They took notes on what they liked and disliked about it. The group took turns at examining the rest of the introduction books. Finally, Tommy placed each person's rating of the books on the blackboard.

Dr. Rob reviewed all the ratings and read over the notes that each one had taken. Two of the books came up with almost the same top rating. He picked up the two books and started scanning his way through them. Dr. Rob was happy to see that he could actually read and understand what was on each page. He was enjoying reading the books and forgot about the others being present.

"Dr. Rob," interrupted the Wizard. "Which book do you think is best for the introductory course?"

"What?" responded Dr. Rob. "Oh, I'm sorry. I was finding out how much fun reading can be. Now about these two books! They both cover the introduction topics well, but I think this book is slightly better." Then Dr. Rob held up one of the books.

"You see," continued Dr. Rob. "The pictures in this book are better and fit in with the text better than this other book. If someone has a little difficulty with reading, the pictures would help reinforce what the book is trying to say. I definitely want this book for the introductory course!"

Everyone agreed with Dr. Rob. Tommy then wrote down the title, author and publisher of the chosen textbook along with the course it should be used for.

The group next moved on to evaluating the pile of textbooks on the history of music.

"I never realized that music had made so many changes over the years," said Tommy. "Perhaps history can be useful at times."

"Well, history is always more interesting when you have a reason for wanting to study it," responded Dorothy. "Reading history just because you are going to have a test on it is not very interesting. Right now you have a purpose for wanting to study the history of music. That makes reading it more interesting to you."

"Being able to read well is fun!" said Katie. "Up until now, I haven't been able to do any real reading for fun. But this has been informative and fun."

"Well, at least you are getting to see what you can look forward to if you learn to read well!" said the Wizard. "You might be surprised at how many people read things just to entertain themselves."

"I have to admit that writing is much more fun when you can spell the words," added Tommy. "It also helps if you have something you really want to write down!"

"Yes, I can see the advantages of being able to read and write well," said Dr. Rob. "I never realized what I have been missing by not being able to read and write. Dorothy, do you really think I can still learn to read and write at my age?"

"Yes you can Dr. Rob," replied Dorothy, "A person can learn to read and write at any age. However, you will have to work hard and be very patient with yourself. Yes, Dr. Rob! You can still learn to read and write."

"Well Dorothy," said the Scarecrow. "It looks like you are having another successful and happy visit to the Land of Oz."

"What else would I expect from a visit to Oz," answered Dorothy. "That's why Oz is known as one of the happy fairy kingdoms. Everything always seems to work out for the best in the end here in Oz."

"Well, I am happy with this trip to Oz," said Dr. Rob. "However, I do want to finish evaluating these books before lunch time."

So the group continued using the same procedures for evaluating the rest of books as they did for the introduction to music book. They were just finishing up with the last stack of books when a student stopped by to tell them that lunch was being served in the dining hall.

Dorothy and her friends had put in a hard morning's work and were ready for lunch. So they followed the students to the dining hall. There was plenty of food. All ate their fill.

Chapter 12 -- The Wizard Helps Katie

As lunch was coming to an end, the Wizard said, "Katie, Professor Wogglebug and I would like to examine your reading skills. We also want to run some other tests on you."

"Will it hurt?" asked Katie.

"No!" replied the Wizard. "It won't hurt a bit. And hopefully we can get at the cause of your reading problem!"

"Okay!" agreed Katie. "Where do you want to do the testing?"

"I think we can use my office," replied Professor Wogglebug. "I have a computer and programs, a good selection of books, and other devices for testing reading abilities."

So Katie, the Wizard and Professor Wogglebug headed for the Professor's office. Once there, the Professor selected an early second grade reading level book for Katie to read.

The Professor handed Katie the book and asked her to start reading it out loud.

"But won't the pill I took this morning still make me read better than I really do?" asked Katie.

"No it won't," replied the Professor. "The pill wore off over an hour ago. If you don't think so, try reading this college level introduction to computer book."

The Professor handed Katie the computer book. Katie tried to read it, but she didn't recognize many of the words. In addition, Katie found the print to be very small.

"I can hardly see the words," said Katie. "And then I don't seem to know what they mean."

"Well, why don't you try this college level book on music?" suggested the Wizard. "You were reading this book earlier this morning."

"Okay," answered Katie, as she took the music book from the Wizard. Katie opened the book and tried to read it. Once again she found the print was small and the words unfamiliar to her.

"You are right, Professor Wogglebug," said Katie. "The reading pill has definitely worn off. Let me try the second grade book."

Once again, the Professor handed Katie the second grade level book. This time she opened it up and started reading it out loud from the beginning. Katie read the book without any problems.

"That was good," said the Professor. "Now let us have you try reading this late second grade level book."

Katie took the new book from the Professor. She opened it up and starting reading it out loud. Once again, Katie had no problems reading the book.

"Well, you can certainly read at the high second grade level," said the Wizard. "Let's have Katie try reading an early third grade reading level book."

The Professor handed Katie another book. Katie opened the book and started reading it. She could read it with some difficulty. As Katie had problems with reading some words, she moved the book closer to her.

"Well, that third grade reading level book does seem to be giving you some problems," said Professor Wogglebug. "Can you tell me why you sometimes move the book closer to you?"

"Sometimes, when I don't quite know a word," replied Katie, "I can figure it out by moving the book closer so I can see it more clearly!"

"Oh!" replied the Wizard. "Professor, could I see that late second grade reading level book and the early third grade reading level book?"

"Of course," replied the Professor. The Professor then handed the Wizard the late second grade book and Katie handed the Wizard the early third grade book.

"Well, isn't this interesting," said the Wizard.

"What is interesting?" asked Katie and the Professor together.

"Why the size of the print of the two books," replied the Wizard. "If you will look carefully at the two books, you will see that the line spacing and print size is slightly smaller on the third grade book!"

"Why so it is!" exclaimed the Professor.

"So what difference does that make?" asked Katie.

"Maybe nothing," answered the Wizard. "But on the other hand it could mean much. Professor Wogglebug, do you happen to have an eye chart?"

"I'm afraid not," replied the Professor. "But my computer does have a vision test program on it!"

"I think that should do nicely," replied the Wizard. "Can we use your computer?"

"No problems," replied the Professor. "Just let me turn the display towards the doorway and then we can pace off twenty feet."

So the Professor turned the computer display toward the doorway. Then he turned on the computer and loaded the vision test program.

While he was doing this, the Wizard carefully measured off twenty feet from the front of the computer display. This took him out into the hallway. He placed a piece of tape on the floor to mark the spot.

"Professor, could I borrow a three by five card from you?" asked the Wizard.

"Of course!" replied the Professor and he handed the Wizard the card.

"Katie, would you come stand behind this tape and face the computer display?" asked the Wizard.

Katie came out into the hallway and stood by the tape.

"Professor," said the Wizard. "If you will now start the program and record the results for us."

"Right!" replied Professor Wogglebug, as he started the vision test program.

The program had Katie cover her left eye and then tell what letters were being displayed on the screen. Each section of the test used smaller letters then the previous section. Next the program requested Katie to cover her right eye and tell what letters were displayed. Finally the program had Katie use both eyes to read the letters on the screen. During all this testing, the Professor was writing down all of Katie's responses. Finally the testing ended and the Wizard and Professor looked over the results.

Professor Wogglebug had Katie sit down at his desk. He handed Katie a book and instructed her to move it closer to herself and then further away from herself until she had the letters of the words just in focus. The Professor then measured the distance between Katie's eyes and the book. He repeated the process with books of different size print.

"Well, how did I do?" asked Katie.

"Well, you seem to be a little near sighted for your age," replied the Wizard. "And your left eye is a little weaker than your right eye."

"So what does that mean?" asked Katie.

"It probably means your reading problem is really a vision problem," replied the Wizard.

"Oh no!" replied Katie. "You can't mean that I need glasses. I am too young to have to wear glasses! I'll just work harder this summer on my reading. I am sure that should take care of the problem."

"Well, let's just have you try reading with a pair of glasses," suggested the Wizard. "Then you can judge for yourself if glasses make reading any easier!"

"All right," agreed Katie. "But the first time one of you calls me four-eyes, I am running away and hiding somewhere where you will never find me!"

"Is that what you do to students in your class that wear glasses?" asked the Professor.

"Well, no I don't," replied Katie. "But many of my classmates do."

Meanwhile, the Wizard was working at the Professor's desk. He had taken some lenses and frames out of his little black bag and was assembling them together. He stopped and took some measurements on Katie's head.

"Katie! What is your favorite color?" asked the Wizard.

"I like yellow best!" replied Katie. "Do I really have to wear glasses? I am going to be an active fifth grader and I am sure the glasses will keep falling off during recess."

"There are some alternatives to wearing glasses. You could try out contact lenses or have an operation on your eyes," replied the Professor. "However, I think you are too young for either of those options."

"Katie, have you ever thought about how glass frames can be a fashion statement?" asked the Wizard. "Do you know some movie actresses wear glass frames with window glass in them just for the fashionable look?"

"Well, I hadn't thought about that!" replied Katie.

"Why glasses can set you off as an individual who is different by choice!" added the Professor. "The proper shape and color of frames and lenses can become your own trade mark!"

"Katie?" asked the Wizard. "Would you please try these glasses on for size?" He handed Katie a pair of glasses with fancy bright yellow frames and pale emerald green lenses.

"Wow!" remarked Katie. "Now these are interesting looking glasses. Where can I find a mirror?"

The Professor found Katie a mirror. She then spent several minutes admiring her new look in the mirror. Finally, the Wizard interrupted Katie's admiring herself.

"Katie," said the Wizard. "Would you try reading the early third grade reading level book again? Read it first without the glasses and then read it with the glasses."

"Okay," agreed Katie. She took off her new glasses, and picked up the third grade reading book. Once again, Katie was able to read the material with great difficulty.

Then the Wizard had Katie put on the glasses and continue reading the book. Katie was able to read the words without difficulty.

"Wow!" said Katie. "It is much easier to read the words when you can see them clearly. Maybe I could learn to like these glasses?"

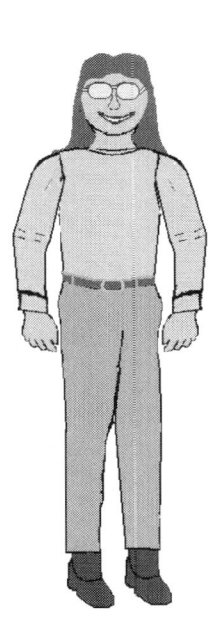

"Why don't you try reading this late third grade reading level book?" suggested Professor Wogglebug. He handed Katie another book.

So Katie started reading the late third grade reading level book. Katie was able to see the words all right. She could even read them without difficulty.

"Now let's try this early fourth grade reading level book," suggested the Wizard.

Once again, Katie was able to see the words clearly. But she read them with difficulty.

"I don't understand," said Katie. "I can see the words and I can pronounce most of the words correctly. Why do I have trouble reading the words?"

"Because you haven't been reading these words before," replied the Wizard. "Your vision problem has slowed down your learning to read. Now that you can see the words clearly, you just need to work on your reading!"

"Perhaps I can lend you some 'fun' third and fourth grade books to read," suggested Professor Wogglebug. "When you run into a word that you don't know, just ask one of us about its pronunciation and meaning. You will be surprised how soon your reading skills will improve."

"Thank you," said Katie, as she took several books from the Professor. "If you are finished with me, I think I'll go show Auntie my new glasses."

"One more thing, before you leave," said the Wizard. "Katie will you please take your glasses off and look out the window at the athletic field. Tell me what you see."

Katie took off her glasses and looked out the window. "I see a soccer game," said Katie. "But the players are kind of far away and hard to see."

"Put your glasses on and look again," said the Wizard.

Katie put on her glasses. "Oh!" responded Katie. "The glasses make the players look sharper. I am able to see the numbers on their uniforms! Number eleven has the ball and is about to pass it to number fourteen."

"I think we are done with you for now, Katie," stated Professor Wogglebug. "We will see you at dinner time. Have fun!"

"Bye Professor! Wizard!" said Katie as she ran out of the room to search for Auntie Dorothy.

Chapter 13 – Tommy's Spelling Problem

Katie found Dorothy and Tommy sitting on a bench next to the athletic fields. She ran up to them and said, "Hi! Notice anything new about me?" Katie really thought the new glasses made her look very unique.

"No!" replied Tommy. "You look like the same old Katie to me!"

"Men!" exclaimed Katie. "They never notice the little things."

"Well, you do seem to be carrying several books," added Tommy.

"Now that's a little better," replied Katie. "I am to try reading these books. However, Auntie, I may need your help with some of the words. Okay?"

"Why don't we read the books after dinner?" suggested Dorothy. "Now wasn't there something else that Tommy hasn't noticed about you yet?"

"Yes there is!" answered Katie.

"Well, I don't see anything else unusual about you," stated Tommy.

"Are you blind?" asked Katie. "Can't you see my new glasses?"

"Glasses?" answered Tommy. "All I see are your yellow and green sun glasses."

They're not sun glasses!" responded Katie. "They are my new fashion statement and reading glasses. Part of my reading problem is a vision problem."

"Well, they are very interesting for reading glasses," agreed Tommy.

"They are very pretty glasses," replied Dorothy. "Won't you sit down and join us? We were just about to discuss Tommy's feelings on spelling."

"Okay!" said Katie and sat down.

"Tommy," said Dorothy. "Would you tell us about your feelings on spelling."

"I just don't understand spelling," said Tommy. "Take the rhyme on how to spell words with ie or ei in them. It goes:
>I before e
>Except after c,
>Or when sounded as a,
>As in neighbor and way.

Now what has the word 'way' got to do with spelling ie and ei words?"

"I believe the word should be 'weigh' as in to find the weight of something," said Katie. "It is not 'way' as in finding your way home."

"I am sure it sounded like 'way' when we were learning the rhyme," replied Tommy.

"Didn't your teacher write the rhyme on the blackboard when you were learning the rhyme?" asked Dorothy.

"I don't remember," replied Tommy.

Katie said, "Well here is what it should have looked like on the blackboard:
>I before e
>Except after c,
>Or when sounded as a,
>As in neighbor and weigh."

"Another thing I really dread doing is to read out loud," said Tommy. "It is okay if I know how to pronounce all the words, but proper names and new words just stop me cold!"

"Why don't you just sound the words out?" asked Katie.

"What do you mean by sound the words out?" replied Tommy.

"You go through the letters of the word and pronounce them phonetically," answered Katie. "After all, the word is just the combination of all the phonemes that make up the word."

"I don't understand," said Tommy. "What do 'phonetically' and 'phonemes' mean?"

"You remember," replied Katie. "In second grade, we learn about phonics, the use of sound symbols in reading. The English language only has 46 sounds or utterances that make up all of our words."

"I can't say that I remember anything about phonics," said Tommy. "I went to second grade before we moved to Eastern Kentucky. They didn't include phonics until third grade at that old school. Here in Eastern Kentucky, our school teaches it in second grade. You may have had phonics, but I didn't!"

"So how do you know how to pronounce a new word?" asked Katie.

"That's simple," replied Tommy. "I get someone to pronounce the word for me, and then I say it over and over. If I am lucky, I have then memorized how to pronounce the word!"

"So you are telling me that you can't sound out a word to figure how to pronounce it?" continued Katie.

"That's about the size of it," answered Tommy.

"I am almost afraid to ask," said Dorothy. "But how do you learn to spell a word?"

"Well, first I try to remember it is pronunciation whenever I see that word," replied Tommy. "Next I simply memorize how to spell the word by repeating its spelling over and over."

"You do know the alphabet?" asked Dorothy.

"Oh yes!" replied Tommy. "It was placed above the blackboard all year in my fourth grade class. I finally memorized it by learning the alphabet song. I can say the words of the song in my head and write the alphabet out for you if you like."

"Another problem I have with spelling is when I am writing a paper in class," continued Tommy. "When I couldn't think of how to spell a word and asked the teacher for help, the teacher always says go look it up in the dictionary."

Katie asked, "So how do you look the spelling of a word up in the dictionary?"

"I don't," replied Tommy. "You have to know how to spell a word before you can find it in the dictionary. If I know how to spell it, I won't need help with the spelling in the first place!"

"Well, you are partly right, Tommy," said Dorothy. "You do need to know how to sound out words so that you can come close to the correct spelling before using the dictionary."

"One thing you can do to improve your spelling is to simply write more," continued Dorothy.

"You could try keeping a diary," suggested Katie. "Then when someone wants to write your biography, all they need to do is refer to your old diaries."

"Why would anyone want to write my biography?" said Tommy. "I have never done anything special."

Dorothy asked, "What about all your visits to the Land of Oz?"

"I forgot about those," replied Tommy. "Anyway, diaries are something that women write, not men!"

"Some men keep diaries," responded Dorothy. "However, if the idea of a diary upsets you, why don't you think about keeping a journal? Men write journals about their scientific works or adventures."

"You think I should try keeping a journal," said Tommy, as he let the idea roll around in his mind. "Just what is a journal?"

"A journal is a summary of what you did," answered Dorothy. "If you are working on some important project, the journal will have all the important steps you have done recorded in it. Journals are very important to engineers, scientists and inventors. You might want to keep a separate journal for each project. What with all your use of computers, you may need to keep a journal about your computer activities."

"Wow!" remarked Tommy. "I think I should start keeping a journal of my activities. You never know when I might do something important!"

"You can have your journal," said Katie. "I think I will just stick with my diary."

"How do I start a journal?" asked Tommy.

"Well, first we need to get you a notebook or two," replied Dorothy. "Next you just sit down and try to write out what you have been doing. For example, you could write down what you remember about our Familyland trip so far. I think I can get you a couple of notebooks from Professor Wogglebug."

"I think that's a great idea," replied Tommy. "When can we get started?"

"We can go looking for the Professor now," replied Dorothy. "There is one thing I need to warn you about, Tommy. You will have to be very patient with yourself at first. You are going to have to ask for help on spelling many of the words. After you have written a page or two of your journal, you can use it to look up spelling for words you use more than once."

"Let's go find Professor Wogglebug!" agreed Tommy with enthusiasm. "What are we waiting for? I want to get started writing my journal right away!" Tommy really found the idea of writing a journal exciting. He could hardly wait for the others to get moving.

"Do either of you know where the Wizard and Professor Wogglebug are, right now?" asked Dorothy.

"I think the Wizard and the Professor are still in the Professor's office," suggested Katie. "If you two will follow me, I will take you there." Katie got up and started for the Professor's office at a semi-run.

So Dorothy and Tommy followed Katie back to the Professor's office. Here they found both the Professor and the Wizard.

"Professor Wogglebug," said Dorothy. "I was wondering if you could do us a favor."

"What can I do for you?" asked Professor Wogglebug.

"Tommy would like to start keeping a journal of his activities," replied Dorothy. "Do you think we could get a notebook or two from you and a couple of pencils?"

"I believe I have some notebooks and pencils in my desk," replied the Professor. "Let me get you a couple of them." The Professor went to his desk and returned with two notebooks, a box of twelve pencils, and a small handheld pencil sharpener. "Will these do?"

"Thank you, Professor!" responded Dorothy. "I think these will do just fine."

"Thank you, Professor Wogglebug!" added Tommy. "This is just what I need. We will see you later."

So Tommy, Katie and Dorothy went back to the bench by the athletic field. Here Tommy tried to start writing his journal.

"How should I start my journal?" asked Tommy.

"I think you need to start with a title page that says: 'This is the Journal of Tommy Gilbert'," responded Dorothy. "Be sure you put today's date on the page as well."

Tommy opened the first notebook and wrote on the first page, "This is the."

"I need help already," said Tommy. "Can one of you spell the word journal for me?"

"The word journal is spelled: J O U R N A L," answered Dorothy.

Tommy finished writing the title: "Journal of Tommy Gilbert." Next he wrote the date on the bottom of the page.

"Now what should I write?" asked Tommy of no one in particular.

"How about, two days ago we went to the airport to catch an airplane to Familyland?" suggested Katie.

"You might want to include the date and times of all the events," suggested Dorothy.

"That sounds good," agreed Tommy, so he turned the page and started writing. This time he could spell all of the words.

Tommy, Katie and Dorothy continued to work on the journal for an hour or two. Finally, it was time for dinner. Tommy put the journal in his quarters and joined the others for dinner.

Chapter 14 -- The Wizard Helps Tommy

As dinner was finishing up, the Wizard asked, "Professor Wogglebug, do you have any computer programs for teaching spelling?"

"Well, we do have some programs in the student computer laboratory for teaching spelling," replied the Professor. "Some of them are games that start off very easy and gradually get more difficult."

"Would you also have any aids for diagnosing spelling problems?" enquired the Wizard.

"Yes, I do have a book or two on that subject," answered the Professor. "Of course I haven't had any need to use those books or programs, since I invented the spelling pill."

"Why can't I just take a spelling pill?" asked Tommy. "That sounds like a nice way to learn spelling!"

"The effects of the pill will wear off when you leave the Land of Oz," replied Professor Wogglebug. "You are from the outside world and need to learn to spell for yourself!"

"Oh!" replied Tommy sadly.

"Tommy," said the Wizard. "If you are done with dinner, why don't we go visit the Professor's office? I would like to see what is causing your spelling difficulty."

"I'm done eating," said Tommy. "Let's go."

So Tommy, Professor Wogglebug and the Wizard went over to the Professor's office. Here the Wizard borrowed a couple of books from the Professor.

"Tommy, why don't you sit at the Professor's desk and try writing down some words as I tell you to?" suggested the Wizard. "One thing first, Tommy, this is not a spelling test. You are not being graded. Just do your best on spelling each word and we will be very happy with you. Okay?"

"I guess that will be all right," said Tommy as he sat down and picked up a pencil and paper. "What shall I write?"

"Why don't you start by writing down your name and address," answered the Wizard. So Tommy wrote down his name and address. This was one thing he could spell without any trouble.

"Can you write out the letters of the alphabet, in order, starting with 'A'?" asked the Professor. So Tommy wrote out the alphabet in all capital letters.

"Now would you write out the alphabet using lower case letters?" asked the Professor. So Tommy wrote out the alphabet in lower case letters.

The Wizard picked up what Tommy had written. "This is very good, Tommy! Now I would like to have you write down some words for me. You just spell them the best that you can."

The Wizard proceeded to have Tommy spell one hundred or so words. Tommy got about one half of the spelling right. Other spellings were close, with one or two letters interchanged such as 'tow' for the number 'two'. He spelled 'run' correctly, but couldn't spell 'ran' or 'running'. Some words were not even close to the correct spelling. In fact, the Wizard would not have had any idea what the words were supposed to be if he had not had the word list in his hands.

"Well Tommy," started the Wizard. "You do have difficulty spelling. Let's have you read some words out loud for me."

Tommy tried to read all the words out loud. Some of them were pronounced correctly. Others were a complete mystery to Tommy. Try as he would, he just couldn't seem to pronounce some of the words.

"Tommy," said the Professor. "You seem to have no pattern to what words you can pronounce and those you can't pronounce. I don't quite understand."

"Let me take a guess at it," suggested the Wizard. "Tommy, how do you learn to pronounce a word?"

"Why I have someone else pronounce it for me," replied Tommy. "Then I try saying it to myself, over and over. Hopefully, I memorize its pronunciation."

"Can't you look at a word and break it into syllables?" asked Professor Wogglebug.

"No I can't," replied Tommy. "Is it important?"

"It is if you are to be able to pronounce words that you have never seen before," replied the Wizard. "Professor, do you have any computer programs for learning phonics?"

"I believe we have some phonics learning programs on the computers in the student computer laboratory," replied

Professor Wogglebug. "I think there are also some programs for learning spelling rules. Why don't we go over to the computer laboratory?"

"Tommy," said the Wizard. "Part of your spelling problem comes from not being able to sound out words. You need to learn phonics. You also need to learn some spelling rules. Lastly, you need to put more time in on practicing spelling."

"The skills of reading, writing, spelling, and pronouncing words all overlap," added Professor Wogglebug. "If you don't work on phonics and spelling rules, you will have trouble with reading and writing. I think we should go over to the student computer laboratory and look at phonics and spelling rules."

"Well, Auntie Dorothy is helping me to start a journal on what I do each day," responded Tommy. "That should give me some writing practice. Also using the words should help me remember how to spell them in the future. But I could use any help you can give me on phonics and spelling rules!"

So Tommy, the Wizard and Professor Wogglebug went over to the student computer laboratory. Here they showed Tommy how to run a phonics program and a spelling program. The programs used games to teach the lessons.

At first, Tommy had a difficult time with the games. He kept losing. Then he started to get the hang of it. "I see that learning phonics and spelling rules, by using games, can almost be fun," exclaimed Tommy.

"Tommy!" said the Wizard. "You like computers, don't you?"

"Well yes," replied Tommy. "I am very fond of computers."

"Then you can use the computer to help you with phonics and spelling," added the Wizard.

"You mean I can play these games on my home computer to learn phonics and spelling?" asked Tommy.

"Well, yes you can do that, Tommy," continued the Wizard. "But you can do other things with the computer. For example, if you kept your journal on your computer using a word-processing program, the program can check your spelling when you are done. You can also buy a talking dictionary program for your computer that can pronounce new words for you. That will help you when you try to read a word you don't know how to pronounce."

"That sounds like a good idea," said Tommy. "Does that mean that I shouldn't write out my journal by hand?"

"No, Tommy!" replied the Professor. "You need to practice writing things out by hand too. You can carry a small notebook with you and write in it anywhere. The computer may not always be that handy."

"Above all else," concluded the Wizard. "You must be patient with your spelling and pronunciation problems. You can't expect them to disappear overnight. It's up to you to overcome your problems. No one else can do it for you."

"You make it sound like my spelling and pronunciation problems are entirely my fault," said Tommy. "But mother and I worked hard on my studying for the spelling tests!"

"The problem isn't any one persons fault," replied Professor Wogglebug. "There are many factors leading up to your problem. However, you are the one who has to solve the problem. Now that you know about your problem, you have to work on fixing it."

"You are showing an interest in the problem," added the Wizard. "Dorothy and your mother want to help you with your problem. The Professor and I can suggest some tools for fixing the problem, but you have to do the work, yourself!"

"Okay," replied Tommy. "I think I understand you. While I am here at the college, I need to visit the computer laboratory, daily and practice my phonics and spelling rules. I also need to write in my journal."

"That's very good Tommy," responded Professor Wogglebug. "Now what are you going to do when you get back home?"

"Why I am going to continue to keep my journal," answered Tommy. "I will also use a word-processor program to record my finished journal entries. However, I will first write things down by hand whenever I think of them. I will also ask my parents to get me a talking dictionary program to help me with pronunciation of words. Finally, Mother, Auntie and I will work on my learning phonics and spelling rules. Does that about cover it?"

"I think that sums up what you need to do, very well," responded the Wizard. "You should also keep in mind that you can write other things than just journal entries. The more you use words, the better your ability will become at reading, writing, spelling and pronouncing them."

"That's great!" said Tommy. "Why don't you let me try these games out for a few more minutes, and then I will call it a day? Thank you for all the suggestions!"

"We were happy to help you, Tommy," said the Wizard. "Have a good evening."

"Good night, Wizard. Good night, Professor Wogglebug," said Tommy, as he went back to playing the phonics and spelling games.

First, Tommy learned that there are vowels and consonants. The vowels are: a, e, i, o, u, and sometimes y. The consonants are: b, c, d, f, g, h, j, k, l, m, n, p, q, r, s, t, v, w, x, y, z.

He also learned that vowels have two different sounds, a short and a long vowel sound. For instance: the 'a' in bat is a short vowel sound, while the 'a' in bate is a long vowel sound. A long vowel sounds says its own name. Also, the ending e in bate is silent!

Chapter 15 -- Katie Practices Reading

While Tommy was working with the Wizard and Professor Wogglebug on finding out the causes of his spelling problem, Katie and Dorothy were in Dorothy's quarters. Katie had brought along the first reading book she borrowed from Professor Wogglebug.

Katie read the title of the book, "The Adventures of Wilbert the Pig." She opened up the book to the first page. Here she found a list of other Wilbert the Pig books.

"Wow!" said Katie. "There must be twenty-five or thirty other books about Wilbert the Pig. And this is the first book in the list of titles. We also have Wilbert as a Detective, Wilbert in the Circus, Wilbert the Texas Ranger, Wilbert as a Pilot, Wilbert Goes to Mars, and many more."

"Well, that's very good," replied Dorothy. "If you like this story, then you know where you can find more stories about Wilbert. The fact that this book is first in the list of titles tells you that it was the first book in the series. That's the best book for you to read first."

Katie turned to the first page of the first chapter and started reading it out loud to Dorothy.

"Wilbert the Pig lives in a little apartment in the side of the barn, just off the barnyard," began Katie. "There is a small porch with a rocking chair on it. The porch faces the barnyard. From there, Wilbert can relax and see everything that goes on in the barnyard."

"Today Wilbert decided to dress up like a farmer," continued Katie. "This morning, he planned to help Farmer James with chores around the farm. The regular hired help had been sick, so the chores weren't getting done."

The book was about the adventures of a pig and his many animal friends from the farm. All the animals could talk and walk about on their hind legs. They had to solve problems much like human beings have. In fact, Wilbert seemed to be superhuman.

"Wilbert was resting in the rocking chair, 'scaring' across the barnyard," continued Katie. "Opps! That does not sound right. Let me try that again."

This time Katie read, "Wilbert was resting in the rocking chair, 'staring' across the barnyard."

"That sounds much better, Katie," encouraged Dorothy. "Remember, even though the words are all in focus, since you got your new glasses, you still need to look at each word carefully. You most read the words that are there on the page, not the words from your imagination."

"I'll try to be more careful in looking at each word," replied Katie. "But at least this time I caught my own error!"

"Yes you did, Katie," complimented Dorothy. "You are doing very well. Shall we continue?"

Katie went back to reading the book.

Dorothy got out some needle-point and started working on it. She was making an Oz map. While Dorothy was working on the needle-point, she listened to Katie's pronunciation of each word.

Whenever Dorothy heard Katie having a problem with a word, Dorothy would help Katie sound out the correct pronunciation. If Katie said a wrong word, Dorothy would have her stop and try it again. She had to keep trying until she got the word correct. Then Katie would reread the entire sentence several times to help her remember the correct pronunciation. Sometimes, Dorothy had to give Katie a hint at how to pronounce a word.

Once in a while, Katie would ask Dorothy what a word meant. Dorothy would then tell Katie what the word meant as it was used in that particular sentence. She would also tell Katie the general meaning of the word.

Katie and Dorothy worked at reading the book for a couple of hours. Finally, Katie finished reading the book.

"I think that is enough reading for today," said Dorothy. "I want you to think reading is fun. You have worked hard enough for one day and did a good job!"

"Well reading is fun, most of the time," replied Katie. "I find it much easier to do now that I can see the words more clearly. I never realized that having to wear glasses could be such fun."

"Well, wearing glasses also has some disadvantages," responded Dorothy. "For one thing, you have to keep them clean if they are going to help your vision. Wearing glasses in a rain storm is no fun! You should also be careful not to break the frames or lenses. And of course you don't want to misplace or lose your glasses!"

"I sure everything has a good and bad side," replied Katie. "But I am surprised that I can like wearing glasses. Do you think we can get together again tomorrow and work on my reading some more?"

"I think we can find some time to work on your reading, tomorrow," answered Dorothy. "We need to practice your reading, everyday for the rest of the summer. Otherwise, you might not be allowed to stay in the fifth grade class in the fall. I know you wouldn't enjoy that."

"I think tomorrow we should start by having you read this story again to me, one more time," continued Dorothy. "That way we can review all the new words you learned today. It will also give you more confidence in your reading ability. Remember, you need to practice reading the words correctly over and over."

"You can also bring along another book for us to read", added Dorothy.

"Do you think I can improve my reading in time for school, this coming fall?" asked Katie.

"I am sure with the aid of some glasses and your mother and me helping you, that you should be ready for fifth grade reading by fall!" responded Dorothy. "If you show half as much interest in reading for the rest of the summer, as you did today, you'll do fine."

"I sure hope so," said Katie. "All my friends are going to be in the fifth grade class. I don't want to go back to fourth grade again!"

"You will do fine!" encouraged Dorothy. "Why don't we call it a day and get some sleep?"

"I think I am ready to go to bed," replied Katie. "I'll see you in the morning. Good night, Auntie!"

"Good night, Katie!" responded Dorothy. "And please don't worry about your reading problems. You made very good progress today. You can expect to continue to improve as long as your work hard at it."

"Well, thank you for all your help and interest, Auntie," said Katie as she ran out of the room.

Katie dreamed about how nice it was to be able to read the college level music textbooks. She also dreamed about being in an adventure with Wilbert the Pig. Her job was to help him out when he encountered reading difficulties. They had a happy time together.

Katie's last dream was about her starting the fifth grade in the fall. She had to read out loud for her new teacher; so that the teacher could decide what reading group Katie belonged in. Suddenly, Katie couldn't remember how to pronounce any of the words. Then the words started spinning around on the page. The words even laughed at Katie.

"You are a fool!" said the words. "You are never going to be able to read us. Being a four-eye isn't going to help you! We'll just get fuzzy and start spinning around the page. You'll never learn to read well!" Then the words started chasing Katie all around the classroom. All the other students looked on in horror!"

Katie woke up screaming, "Help! The words are after me!" She had broken out in a cold sweat."

Katie turned on the light. It was just about time for Katie to be getting up anyway. She decided to go ahead and get up and get dressed. Her last dream had really shaken her up.

There was only one thing for Katie to do. She got out the book that she and Auntie Dorothy had read the night before. Katie started reading the book from the first page of the first chapter.

"Wilbert the Pig lives in a little apartment in the barn, just off the barnyard," read Katie out loud. "He had many animal friends in the barnyard."

"Wow! What a relief!" thought Katie. "The dream was just a bad nightmare. I can still read this book."

Katie continued reading the book until a student came and told her it was time for breakfast. So Katie put away the book and headed for the dining hall.

Chapter 16 – Plans For the Music Program

Dorothy, Katie, Tommy, Dr. Rob, the Scarecrow, and the Wizard, all gathered together at the dining hall for breakfast. Once again, Professor Wogglebug joined them.

"I am delighted with your progress so far on organizing the music department," said Professor Wogglebug. "What do you think you want to do today?"

"I think we should be able to finish the design of the music program, today," responded Dr. Rob. "Maybe this evening, I could conduct tryouts for some barber shop quartets and beauty shop quintets?"

"That's sounds great," replied the Professor. "I'll announce the tryouts in a few minutes. I'll also have posters put up before lunch time. By the way, you will each find pills by your water glasses. These will allow you to read and spell well for the rest of the morning."

"Thank you, Professor," replied Dr. Rob. "I can use all the help I can get when it comes to reading. When do you think you can help me out with my reading problem?"

"I believe the Professor and I would like to see you after lunch," said the Wizard. "It will probably take us all afternoon to find out your problem. After that, we will try to tell you how to overcome your problem."

"I'll be looking forward to this afternoon," said Dr. Rob. "Meanwhile, I plan to enjoy being able to read again for this morning."

"Dr. Rob. What's a barber shop quartet?" asked Tommy.

"A barber shop quartet is a group of four men singing in harmony," replied Dr. Rob.

"And what is a beauty shop quintet?" asked Katie.

"Why a beauty shop quintet is a group of five women singing in harmony," responded Dr. Rob. "After all, why should men have all the fun?"

Professor Wogglebug went off and announced the tryouts for barber shop quartets and beauty shop quintets for that evening. The group finished eating breakfast. Next they went next door to the music classroom.

They worked all morning on finishing the curriculum and course outlines for the music program. There were detailed plans for a Music Conductor degree and a Music Instructor degree program.

"I think we have a good music program planned for the college," said Dr. Rob. "Thank you, Tommy, for taking such good notes."

"Taking notes is easy if you know how to spell the words," replied Tommy. "I only hope I can learn to spell this well on my own someday. So what else do we need to do today for the music program?"

"I think I need to look over those stacks of sheet music," replied Dr. Rob. "I'll need some music for tonight's tryouts. Do any of you have any ideas for songs for the quartets and quintets?"

"I don't think any of us have been in a quartet or quintet," answered Dorothy. "Well, maybe that's not quite right. The Scarecrow, the Tin Woodman, the Cowardly Lion and I once sang a song as a group of four on our way to the Emerald City to ask the Wizard for help. I guess that was a quartet."

"You would have to call that a mixed quartet," added the Scarecrow. "It certainly wasn't made up of four men."

"The Scarecrow is right, Dorothy," agreed Dr. Rob. "You were in a mixed quartet, not a barber shop quartet. We may try to form a mixed quartet or two if the students are interested."

"Anyway," continued Dr. Rob. "We need songs that have four or five part harmony written for them. So now I need to search through the stacks of sheet music looking for songs that might work for a quartet or quintet."

"Wouldn't it also help if you had a group to demonstrate a quartet and quintet song for this evening?" asked Katie. "Perhaps they could give a short demonstration at dinner time?"

"That would be nice," replied Dr. Rob. "But where am I going to find such a group?"

"Well, there are five of us here," replied Tommy. "Isn't that enough for either a quartet or a quintet?"

"I don't know," replied Dr. Rob. "What song do you know that might work for a quartet or a quintet? I mean we really don't have much time to prepare for tonight."

Tommy and Katie got their heads together for a few moments. Then Katie announced, "Why not use the song: 'What is Oz without Ozma?' We sang the song with Auntie Dorothy on our first trip to Oz."

"And the Scarecrow has heard the song played by the Royal Court Band," added Tommy. "Now if you will help us learn to harmonize the song, we can perform it at dinner tonight."

"That is, if it is all right with Auntie Dorothy and the Scarecrow?" added Katie.

"It's fine with me," responded the Scarecrow.

"I can be used to make it a quintet," added the Wizard. "That is if you can find a song with five parts."

"Well, let me take a look at the stacks of music for a few minutes," replied Dr. Rob. "Then we can practice a song for the quartet and one for the quintet." So Dr. Rob spent a few minutes looking over the stack of sheet music.

"We are in luck!" exclaimed Dr. Rob. "I found the sheet music for: 'What is Oz without Ozma?' And it has four harmonized parts! We can practice it first."

"I also found a copy of the music for: 'Sweet Adeline' with five part harmony," continued Dr. Rob. "That will give us something for your quintet to sing."

"That's great," replied Dorothy. "The Scarecrow, Katie, Tommy and I can start practicing: 'What is Oz without Ozma?' I know the Wizard has heard this song before. It is a favorite of the Royal Court Band. It was written after Ozma became the ruler of all of Oz. That was after the Wizard gave up being the ruler of Oz."

"Well, yes Dorothy!" said the Wizard. "I have heard the song played by the Royal Court Band. I believe I have even heard some of the citizens in the Emerald City sing the words to the song. It has been a long time since I was ruler of Oz. I was glad to let other people take over the responsibility. Back then, I wasn't even a good wizard. I was just a fake or a humbug."

"Well, maybe you were a humbug," agreed Dorothy. "But you were able to help out the Tin Woodman, the Cowardly Lion, and the Scarecrow."

"You also encouraged us to get rid of the Wicked Witch of the West," added the Scarecrow. "That set free many people from her power."

"True," agreed the Wizard. "But I still wasn't able to send Dorothy home."

"Well, I guess I'll just sit here and listen while Dr. Rob helps you learn to do four part harmony," finished the Wizard, as he sat down in a chair.

"Let me get a pitch pipe from the musical instrument cupboard," said Dr. Rob. "And we can get started on the harmony." Dr. Rob walked over to the cupboard and got out a pitch pipe.

"Okay now," said Dr. Rob. "We need to choose parts for the quartet. I think we will give Katie the soprano part, Dorothy will do the alto, Tommy will do tenor, and the Scarecrow will do the bass part. In this arrangement, the alto part has the melody. That means Dorothy's part will have the recognized part of the song."

"Well, that only fair," said the Scarecrow. "After all, it was Dorothy's adventure."

"Let me play the starting note for each of your parts," said Dr. Rob. "Then you need to hum that note." So Dr. Rob played the notes on his pitch pile and each singer hummed their note.

"Now if we can have all of you hum your note at the same time," said Dr. Rob. So Dorothy, Katie, Tommy and the Scarecrow hummed their first note of the song. It made up a musical cord.

"That was good," said Dr. Rob. "Now we need to practice each part separately. We will start with Dorothy's part, since it carries the melody." Dr. Rob then helped Dorothy go through her part. Since Dorothy already knew the song, it didn't take long.

"Now we will try to practice Katie's part," continued Dr. Rob. "It's too bad you don't read music or you could just sing the top line of notes on this sheet."

"But Dr. Rob," said Katie. "I am still under the influence of that reading pill. I think I can even read music!" So Katie read the notes that Dr. Rob pointed to and then she sang the words.

"That was good!" replied Dr. Rob. "Now let's have Dorothy and Katie sing their parts together." Dorothy and Katie sang their parts together.

"Wow!" exclaimed Tommy. "Adding a second part to the song does make it more interesting!"

"Good!" replied Dr. Rob. "In that case, let's try out your part. Do you think you can read this music?"

"I was reading college books," replied Tommy. "How hard can it be to read music?" So Tommy and Dr. Rob worked on Tommy's part of the song. Next, Tommy, Katie, and Dorothy all sang their parts together. It was even more beautiful than the duet by Katie and Dorothy.

Finally, Dr. Rob and the Scarecrow worked on the bass part. When they had it down cold, then Dorothy, Katie, Tommy and the Scarecrow tried doing all their parts together.

"That was wonderful!" said the Wizard. "I never knew you thought so highly of Ozma."

"Well, Wizard," said Dr. Rob. "Now it's your turn. You are going to sing the baritone part of this song. It is the melody for Sweet Adeline."

So the group practiced doing Sweet Adeline. Finally, it was time for lunch.

Chapter 17 -- The Wizard Helps Dr. Rob

Everyone went to the dining hall for lunch. They were joined by Professor Wogglebug.

"How is the planning for my music department coming?" asked the Professor.

"I think we got that task pretty well finished," replied Dr. Rob. "We were also able to rehearse a quartet and quintet song for tonight. Hopefully that will get some students interested in the music program. I think tomorrow we can let students drop by and try out some of the musical instruments."

"Now I am sure that getting to try out some of the instruments will be of great interest to the students," replied Professor Wogglebug. "Of course your demonstration of the quartet and quintet will also be a hit."

"I am sure we will have fun doing the demonstration," said Dr. Rob. "Now what shall we do for this afternoon?"

"If it is all right with all of you," said Tommy. "I think I will go to the student computer laboratory and practice phonics and spelling rules."

"And I would like to practice reading with Auntie," added Katie.

"I think that would be a good idea, Katie and Tommy," replied Dorothy. "What do you have planned for this afternoon, Dr. Rob?"

"I believe the Wizard and I have plans for Dr. Rob," said Professor Wogglebug. "We want to take a look at his reading problem."

"In that case, we can all get back together here for dinner," said the Wizard as he got up from the table. So everyone went their own way.

Professor Wogglebug and the Wizard led Dr. Rob to the Professor's office. Here they set about trying to discover the source of Dr. Rob's reading problem.

"Let's start with you reciting the alphabet," said the Wizard.

Dr. Rob was able to say the alphabet without any trouble.

"Now that was fine," said Professor Wogglebug, "Now can we ask you to write out the alphabet in order from 'a' to 'z'."

Dr. Rob wrote out the alphabet in mixed upper and lower case letters. He also made the letters e and h written backwards.

"Could you write the alphabet in all upper case letters?" asked the Wizard.

Dr. Rob had trouble remembering how to write the alphabet in all upper case letters. It took him several minutes to complete the task. This time, he wrote the letter N backwards.

"Now let's try writing the alphabet in all lower case letters," continued the Professor.

This time Dr. Rob took five minutes to complete the task. He wrote the letters 'a' and 'g' backwards.

"Would you mind writing out your name, address and telephone number?" asked the Wizard.

Dr. Rob was able to do that quickly.

"And do you know your social security number?" added Professor Wogglebug.

So Dr. Rob wrote out his social security number.

"Can you write down some more words that you can spell," asked the Wizard.

Dr. Rob wrote out twenty unrelated words. They included, dog, cat, hot dog, pizza, and so forth.

"So you can do some minimum reading and writing," said the Wizard.

"Well, I do have to be able to give people my name, address and telephone number from time to time," replied Dr. Rob. "But I won't say that I can really read or write."

"I understand that you have a driver's license," continued the Wizard. "If that is correct, then you recognize up to another 164 words and phrases related to driving."

"Well, I recognized the words and phrases on the sign test for the driver's license test," replied Dr. Rob. "But it didn't cover nearly that many words."

"Why don't we try having you read a first grade book?" suggested Professor Wogglebug. He handed Dr. Rob the book. The book was 'Fun with Dorothy and Toto.'

Dr. Rob opened the book and started reading it slowly. "Why I remember this book from when I was in first grade," remarked Dr. Rob. He then began to recite the book from memory. "Dorothy. See Dorothy. See Dorothy run."

"Well, now we know how you got by your reading lessons in grade school," said the Wizard. "With a memory like yours, you only had to hear the teacher or one of the other students read it out loud once. Then when it was your turn to read, you recited it from memory."

"I do believe your good memory worked against your learning to read," added the Professor. "You find it simpler to repeat the words from memory than to read the words."

"Maybe we can use your memory to help you learn to read?" suggested the Wizard. "Why don't we try having you point to each word in the book as you recite them? After all, that is how we learn to read by sight."

Dr. Rob then pointed to each word as he recited the book from memory. He found out that he could follow the words.

"While you were reading, or if you prefer reciting, that book," said Professor Wogglebug, "I was making a list of the words in that story. I want you to repeat your reading of that book twice more. Then let's see how many of the words you can recognize by themselves."

So Dr. Rob 'read' through the book again and again. Then he took the Professor's reading test.

"That's amazing," said Dr. Rob. "You mean to tell me that I can learn to read some words that easily?"

"Well, you do know how to read more words that you think you do," replied the Wizard. "And you probably really learned to read these few words back in first grade! However, you will require many hours of work to become a functioning adult reader. It won't be easy or all fun. It will be hard work."

"You not only need to learn to read," added Professor Wogglebug. "But you also need to learn to write, spell, and pronounce written words."

"You mean I need to study phonics and spelling rules like Tommy," replied Dr. Rob. "Oh, and I also needed to start writing a journal."

"Well, you do need to do all of that," continued the Professor. "But you are not ready for what Tommy is doing yet. Tommy is about five grades ahead of you in reading and writing skills. No, you need to start reading lesson from scratch."

"You need to get professional help!" said the Wizard. "There are several organizations that want to help you with your reading problem. For example: Adult Basic Education, Literacy Volunteers of America, and Literacy Action, Inc. I am sure Dorothy can find local telephone numbers for you when you get back home."

"But if I go to one of those organizations, someone will probably find out that I can't read!" said Dr. Rob. "I could lose my job!"

"Actually, most people will be willing to help you out with your reading problem," said the Professor. "They will think you are very brave to learn to read at your age. But you are right; some people may look down on you while you are trying to learn to read. That problem will go away, once you improve your reading skills."

"While you are here in Oz," continued the Wizard, "we can work on your reading. With a lot of luck and hard work, we can get you through a grade level or two. However, the higher your reading skills get, the slower will be your advance in grade levels."

"We are talking about you needing months or more likely years of work to completely overcome your problem!" finished Professor Wogglebug. "If you are willing, we can start working on reading, spelling, and writing right now."

So Dr. Rob spent the next couple of hours 'reading' his old first grade books. Next, the Professor would have him read the single words off of flash cards. Finally the Wizard gave him a simple spelling test. It was a long and exhausting afternoon for Dr. Rob.

By dinner time, Dr. Rob was surprised at how many words he could actually recognize. What with all the television commercials and neon signs, Dr. Rob actually had a reading vocabulary of several hundred words. Of course these include words like taco, hot dog, hamburger, pizza, ice cream, candy, tide, and so forth. These were not all words that would be included in a first or second grade reading list.

"That was one exhausting session," said Dr. Rob. "But I am happy to say I can read a little bit. That sounds better than saying I can't read at all."

"Yes, this session was a lot of work," added the Wizard. "And just think that you can look forward to doing this daily for the next few years!"

Dr. Rob asked, "How long before I can start reading things on my own?"

"You will need to learn five hundred to one thousand basic words before you can begin to be a functionally literate adult," replied the Wizard.

"Well, you need to be a sixth grade reader to understand the driver's license manual," stated Professor Wogglebug. "It takes an eighth grade reader to understand the instructions on a frozen TV dinner or the directions on an aspirin bottle."

"By the time you get to a twelfth grade reading level, you should be able to understand a newspaper," added the Wizard. "However, you can start looking at newspapers and circling the words you know now!"

"Thank you for all your help," said Dr. Rob. "Can we get together and do some more of this tomorrow?"

"We would be happy to do that," said Professor Wogglebug. "Now let's go eat dinner."

So the professor, the Wizard, and Dr. Rob went to the dining hall.

Chapter 18 -- The Singing Demonstration

Katie, Tommy, Dorothy and the Scarecrow were waiting at the Professor's table in the dining hall, when the Wizard, Professor Wogglebug and Dr. Rob got to the dining hall.

"Hello," said Dorothy. "I hope you had a good afternoon."

"I sure did," replied Dr. Rob. "But it was hard work!"

"Oh!" responded Dorothy. "And how did the Professor and Wizard do with you reading problem?"

"Well, they seem to think that my good audio memory got in the way of my learning to read," replied Dr. Rob. "It seems that I remember the words from my first grade reading books. Now they are hoping that I can use my memory to learn my first grade reading lessons. Basically, I need to learn reading from scratch!"

"Oh dear!" replied Dorothy. "That could take a long time!"

"Months to years," replied Dr. Rob. "But I did find out that I already know some words. From now on, I just have to work hard at reading every chance I get!"

"Well, I have to practice spelling, phonics, and writing several times a day," said Tommy. "This afternoon, I wrote in my journal and worked on phonics in the computer laboratory."

"Auntie helped me practice reading this afternoon," added Katie. "Now, I can read all the words in the first book correctly!"

"I am glad to see we are all working on our problems," added Dr. Rob. "Are you all ready to demonstrate the quartet and quintet after dinner?"

"Well, I think we are a little nervous about that performance," answered Dorothy. "How are you two doing Katie and Tommy?"

"Doing anything in front of a large group of people always makes me nervous," said Katie.

"Me too!" added Tommy. "I think I am going to be sick."

"You'll be alright once you start singing," said Dr. Rob. "It's the waiting around that is hard on you."

"If you are sick, then I guess you won't want any dessert?" suggested Dorothy.

"Maybe I might be able to eat a little dessert," replied Tommy. "After all, I need to keep up my strength."

"Well, you better limit it to just one dessert for now," added Dr. Rob. "You don't want to be over full just before you do a performance. I am sure we can find you, something to snack on after the performance."

"Okay! Whatever you think is best," agreed Tommy, as he helped himself to a piece of Oz pie.

Katie asked, "So how soon will we be performing? What do I do if I forget the words?"

"Well, the best way to get over your nervousness is to get the show started," replied Dr. Rob. "If you are done eating, I suggest that we all go over to the stage and get ready. I placed copies of the sheet music on the chairs on the stage. The sheet music includes the words to the songs. It's all right to look at the words, while you are singing the songs. However, try to keep one eye on me!"

"What are we waiting for? Let's get this show started," said Dorothy. "Come on everyone, follow me!" So Dorothy bravely led the way to the stage, with the Scarecrow, the Wizard, Tommy, Katie, Dr. Rob, and Professor Wogglebug following her. Dr. Rob and the five singers sat down on the chairs on the stage.

"Are my knees suppose to be knocking together like this?" asked Katie.

"That's a perfectly normal response to being up in front of a group," replied Dorothy. "Performing gets easier to do the more you do it."

Professor Wogglebug walked up to the center of five microphones at the front of the stage. "Ladies and Gentlemen," said the Professor. "Tonight, for your enjoyment, Dr. Rob and some of his friends are going to demonstrate a mixed quartet and quintet. It is my pleasure to introduce Dr. Rob. He will introduce his group of singers. Then they will give a demonstration of the quartet and quintet. If any of you are interested in learning to sing like this, please see me or Dr. Rob after the performance."

Dr. Rob began by introducing Dorothy, Katie, Tommy, the Scarecrow and the Wizard. "We will start with a quartet featuring Katie singing soprano, Dorothy singing alto, Tommy singing tenor, and the Scarecrow singing bass," continued Dr. Rob. These four gathered around Dr. Rob who then got out his pitch pipe. He played the starting notes for each part of the quartet song, 'What is Oz without Ozma?'

The dining hall became dead quiet in anticipation of what was to come. Then Dorothy, Katie, Tommy and the Scarecrow started singing. Dorothy made the melody come alive. Katie was marvelous as a soprano. Tommy did great with the tenor part. The Scarecrow was unbeatable with the bass part. They sounded fabulous together.

> **What is Oz without Ozma**

They sang their way through four verses of the song. When they finished singing the last verse, there was silence in the dining hall. Then the students broke out into loud applause. It took several minutes to quiet the crowd down so the performance could continue.

This time, the Wizard joined the singers to make it a quintet. He was going to sing the baritone part of the harmony. They began singing the song 'Sweet Adeline.' The Wizard's baritone lead was fantastic. This time they presented five verses. When they finished, the hall grew quiet once more. Finally, the students gave the singers a standing ovation.

After several minutes of applause, a student got up and shouted, "Encore!" This was quickly followed by more students shouting, "Encore! Encore!" Next, the students started stamping their feet and continued to shout, "Encore!"

Professor Wogglebug went to the microphone and asked for quiet. "I will ask Dr. Rob if they have any more songs ready. But I believe that they only had time to prepare the performance of these two songs. Dr. Rob?"

"I'm sorry," said Dr. Rob. "But we only had time to prepare the two songs. We have only been working on it since this morning. If you like, we can repeat the performance of these two songs."

"Yes! Yes!" replied the students as they applauded again.

So they repeated the performance of, 'What is Oz without Ozma?' and 'Sweet Adeline.' When they finished singing, they received another standing ovation. By now, Tommy, Katie, Dorothy, the Wizard, the Scarecrow and Dr. Rob were actually enjoying themselves.

Once Dr. Rob had gotten the hall quiet once more, he said, "What you just heard were mixed quartet and quintet singing. We will also like to form some all men and all women singing groups. Of course each group will learn a full selection of songs. And if you like, we can even have a singing competition in the near future!"

All the students liked the idea of a singing competition. Many of the students came up to the stage. They asked Dr. Rob and Professor Wogglebug about how they could learn to sing in a quartet or quintet. The Professor made a list of their names. He promised that they could begin their singing lessons at ten the next morning. He also announced that there would be try outs for the quartets and quintets at that time.

"And don't forget to drop by the music classroom, tomorrow morning, and try out some of the musical instruments," concluded Professor Wogglebug. "Have a good evening."

"Wow! I'm glad that's over," said Tommy. "I feel much better now. It was almost fun singing in front of that group. Now if I can just find myself a snack."

Professor Wogglebug went and got Tommy several donuts. Tommy thanked the Professor.

"At least we had company for our performance," said Dorothy. "Think how much harder it would have been if you were singing a solo. Of course this experience is going to make its way into your journal?"

"That's right," replied Tommy. "I do need to make some entries for today. Singing in harmony will make a good topic. I will also make a note about what it feels like to be up on a stage in front of a group of people."

"They call it stage fright," said Katie. "The only way to get over stage fright is to keep on getting up in front of groups."

"Even if you do perform in front of groups all the time, you may still be nervous just before you get started," added Dorothy. "Once you get into the performance, you forget about the stage fright."

"Well, I don't know about you two, but I have had enough excitement for today," said Katie. "I'll see you all in the morning."

"Good night!" said everyone to each other. Each of them went to his or her quarters. Tommy wrote in his journal for about thirty minutes. Then he got ready for bed. Within an hour, all of them were fast asleep.

Chapter 19 – Trying the Musical Instruments

Everyone got up, got dressed, and ate breakfast. The breakfast included reading and spelling pills. Next, they all gathered in the music classroom. Here, Dr. Rob began to get out all of the musical instruments and try them out.

"Can you really play all of these musical instruments?" asked Tommy. "I mean, I can't even play one of them."

"I can show you how to play each of these instruments," replied Dr. Rob. "But I can't play all these instruments all that well."

"However, I think there are some instruments here that you can play without having to learn how," added Dr. Rob. "Why don't you try this one?" Then Dr. Rob handed Tommy a triangle and a striker.

"Okay, you win, Dr. Rob," responded Tommy. "I guess I can play a triangle." Tommy struck the triangle so he could hear its tone.

"What instruments do you think I could play?" asked Katie.

"Well, I have a little more difficult instrument for you to try," Dr. Rob. "Here, try this." Dr. Rob handed Katie two cymbals.

"These look easy to use," said Katie as she clanged them together. The cymbals gave off a clang and then stopped making noise.

"As you see," said Dr. Rob, "those are harder to use than they look. You must give them a glancing blow motion so that each cymbal can continue to vibrate."

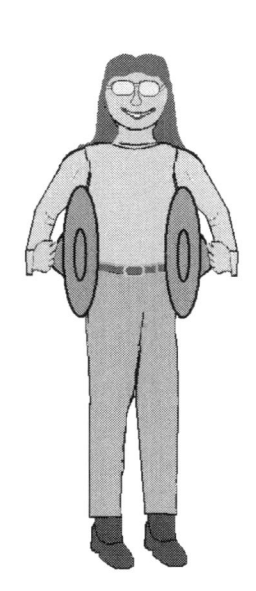

So Katie tried giving the cymbals a glancing blow. This time, the cymbals continued to ring for several seconds.

"Tommy," suggested Dr. Rob. "Why don't you pretend to be the chimes of a clock, and it is just four o'clock?" So Tommy struck the triangle four times.

"What other instruments have you got that we can try playing?" asked Katie.

"Well, we have a drum set over there," said Dr. Rob. He then walked over to the drum set. Dr. Rob sat down on a stool in the middle of it. "As you can see, the cymbals are worked by this pedal. Or you can use a drum stick. This gives you better control than just hitting the two cymbals together." Next, Dr. Rob worked the pedal a couple of times. This was followed by striking the cymbals several times using drum sticks.

"Now the bass drum is controlled by this second pedal," continued Dr. Rob. He beat the drum three times. "Of course you could work the bass drum by hitting it with a large drum stick." He picked up a large drum stick and beat the bass drum with it.

"The two snare drums here require striking with small drum sticks," continued Dr. Rob. "It looks very easy to strike the snare drums. But it isn't. It will take considerable practice to get the proper feel to it." Dr. Rob then proceeded to play a short number on the drum set. He showed good rhythm and made considerable noise.

This attracted the attention of some of the students walking by. They came into the room and joined Tommy and Katie in watching Dr. Rob play the drums.

When Dr. Rob had finished his number, he said, "As I said, I am not very good on the drums. But that should give you some idea of how it works. The hardest part is learning to play the snare drums. I have four snare drums around here somewhere. If I can just find them then you can try them out for yourselves." So Dr. Rob found the four snare drums and four sets of drum sticks.

Three students and Tommy volunteered to try out the snare drums. Katie decided she would try out the drum set. Dr. Rob spent the next several minutes showing everyone how hold the drum sticks. To work properly, one has to hold them loosely. Everyone tried beating their drum for several minutes. Of course Katie also beat the bass drum and struck her cymbals.

"Why don't we try out the glockenspiels next?" suggested Dr. Rob.

"What's a glockenspiel?" asked Katie.

"Why a glockenspiel is sort of a small xylophone that you can carry around with you," replied Dr. Rob. "I have four of them over here. You play them by striking the keys with these small hammers. Let me place this strap around my neck and I'll show you how it is played."

Dr. Rob proceeded to pick up a glockenspiel, fastened the strap around his neck and starting playing. He played 'Happy Birthday' and 'Twinkle, Twinkle Little Star.'

"That looks like fun," said several students. "Can we try that?"

"Sure thing," replied Dr. Rob. "We'll just help you on with the glockenspiels and then you just watch me and hit the same keys. I will take it slowly at first."

So the three students put on their glockenspiels and picked up their hammers. Dr. Rob went through 'Twinkle, Twinkle Little Star' very slowly several times. Next, the students followed along after him several times. Finally they were able to play the song at its regular speed.

"Now we can proceed to the more difficult stringed instruments," said Dr. Rob. "Here we have the harp, ukulele, the guitar, the violin, the cello, and the bass fiddle."

"As you can see," continued Dr. Rob, "it is very easy to get noise out of a ukulele or guitar. It takes many hours of practice to learn to control the finger positions and thus turn the noise into music. Of course you also have the problem of tuning the instrument before you use it each time." So Dr. Rob demonstrated the ukulele and the guitar.

"The violin, cello and bass fiddle are generally played using a bow," said Dr. Rob. "The bow also must be adjusted before each use. You also need to put rosin on the bow strings to give them a better grip on the violin strings. Once again, one needs to learn the finger position." Dr. Rob then demonstrated the violin, cello and bass fiddle.

The students, Katie and Tommy, took turns trying out each of the instruments. They were able to make lots of noise, but very little music.

"Now let's move on to the brass wind instruments," suggested Dr. Rob. "There we have the trumpet, the French horn, the baritone, the trombone, the tuba, and the sousaphone. Since the trumpet is the easiest to play, we will start with it." So Dr. Rob played a few notes on the trumpet.

Tommy tried to blow a note on the trumpet. But all he got was the sound of rushing air. Katie and the students didn't do any better.

"It's not that easy to play a note on a brass wind instrument," said Dr. Rob. "It is necessary that you make your lips buzz like this:" He then buzzed his lips a few times. "It also requires good lungs."

Tommy tried buzzing his lips. After several tries, he succeeded. Then he tried to play the trumpet again. This time he produced a clear note.

"Now try changing the value positions and play the trumpet again," said Dr. Rob.

So Tommy moved one of the values and played the trumpet again. This time, he sounded a different note. Katie and the students tried the trumpet again. This time, a few of them were more successful.

"Now let's finish up with the wood winds," said Dr. Rob. "These include the flute, clarinet, saxophone and bassoon. Except for the flute, you have a wood reed that you have to make vibrate to produce the sounds in these instruments. In the case of the flute, you must blow across this hole in such a way that you make it whistle. This is something like blowing across the top of an empty pop bottle and making it whistle." Dr. Rob then demonstrated the wood wind instruments.

Tommy, Katie and the students each tried out the wood wind instruments. For the most part, they were not successful in producing any sound.

"We do have one more instrument, that all of you can make play," said Dr. Rob. "It is the piano, a percussion stringed instrument." So Dr. Rob concluded his tour of the musical instruments with the piano. He sat down and played several songs on it.

"Now if some of you would like to try out the piano, you can do a duet with me," suggested Dr. Rob. "I will show you how to play the harmony for 'Chop Sticks' while I do the melody."

Katie, Tommy and the students all took Dr. Rob up on his offer. It only took Dr. Rob several minutes to teach them to do the harmony. Finally, each of them got to play a duet with Dr. Rob.

"That was fun!" said Tommy and Katie together.

"We had a most enjoyable time," added the students.

"Isn't it about time for the quartet and quintet try outs," asked one of the students. "That is this morning, isn't it?"

Chapter 20 – Try-outs for the Singing Groups

"You are right!" replied Dr. Rob. "It is time for the quartet and quintet try outs. Tommy, why don't you check out in the hallway and see if anyone is waiting there?"

"Sure thing, Dr. Rob," replied Tommy. He went out into the hallway. Here he found a group of men and women students waiting for the try outs.

"Why didn't you go on in?" asked Tommy.

"We didn't want to disturb your music lessons," replied one student. "They did sound very interesting."

"It was very interesting," replied Tommy. "I am sure that if you will ask Dr. Rob, that he will be willing to repeat the musical instrument demonstration tomorrow."

"We'll have to ask Dr. Rob about that," said one of the students. "If you are sure he won't mind."

"I am sure he will be happy to do it for you," answered Tommy. "Now it is time for the quartet and quintet try outs. Come on, let's all go inside." So the students followed Tommy into the classroom.

"Dr. Rob," said Tommy. "These students are here for the quartet and quintet try outs. They would also like you to repeat the musical instrument demonstrations again tomorrow."

"I'd be happy to repeat the musical instrument demonstration, tomorrow morning," replied Dr. Rob.

"Welcome to the try outs for the quartets and quintets," said Dr. Rob. "We need to divide you up into groups of altos, sopranos, tenors, basses, and baritones. A quartet will consist of an alto, a soprano, a tenor, and a bass singer. A quintet will consist of an alto, a soprano, a tenor, a baritone, and a bass singer."

"The first thing I need to have each of you do for me is to sing some musical scales," continued Dr. Rob. "This is how I will judge which of you should sing soprano, alto, tenor, baritone, and bass. After that, you can all get together and choose members from each of the four or five groups that make up a quartet or quintet. If you will please form a single line, we can get started!"

So the students lined up.

"Okay, then," continued Dr. Rob, to the first student in line. "I will play the notes of a scale. Then I want you to sing the scale by singing: 'do,' 're,' 'mi,' 'fa,' 'so,' 'la,' 'ti,' 'do.' We will repeat the process with several different scale ranges. Are you ready?"

"I'm ready, Dr. Rob," said the first student.

So Dr. Rob played a scale on the piano. Then the student sang the scale. This was repeated for several octaves of the scale, until Dr. Rob find the limits to the singer's range.

Next, Dr. Rob played some isolated notes and asked the student to sing each note. Finally, Dr. Rob finished testing the first student and made his decision on which group to place the student in. This student was placed in the soprano singer group.

Dr. Rob repeated the process for all of the students. After about one hour of work, Dr. Rob had the students divided into the five groups.

Next, the students all got together and formed quartets and quintets. They formed five barber shop quartets, four beauty shop quintets and one mixed quintet. Where possible, the students chose to make up a group from friends. The mixed quintet was made up out of all the left over students. They didn't even know one another. It was either be in the mixed quintet or not get to participate. It also gave them all a chance to make new friends.

Dr. Rob had each group choose a name for itself. He then made a list of the group names along with the members of each group.

Each quartet was made up of singers from only a single region of Oz. They were called: the Munchkin Farmers, the Quadling Magicians, the Winkie Foresters, the Gillikin Sorcerers, and the Emerald City Singers.

The beauty shop quintets each came from a single region of Oz. They were called: the Munchkin Beauties, the Gillikin Hair Dressers, the Winkie Stylists, and the Quadling Debutantes.

The mixed quintet was called the Oz Mixed Quintet and was made up of members from each of the four countries of Oz and one student from the Emerald City.

"I have a stack of songs here for quartets," said Dr. Rob. "And here is another stack of songs here for quintets. I would like each of your groups to look over the appropriate stack of songs. Each group should choose their favorite three songs, or at least the songs they like most. If you need me to, I can play some of the songs for you."

The groups looked at the sheet music. Many of the songs were new to them. Others were not. Dr. Rob was busy playing the unfamiliar songs on the piano. By lunch time, all the groups had chosen three songs that they liked.

"Dr. Rob," asked one of the students. "Will we be wearing special outfits or uniforms for the competition? I mean, like haven't I heard of barber shop quartets dressing up like barbers and customers?"

"Yes, you may have heard or seen a barber shop quartet dressed up like barbers and customers. However, there is no reason why all of the quartets and quintets groups need to dress alike," responded Dr. Rob. "So this is one more thing for you to think about before you leave. Each group needs to be thinking about what costumes they want to wear for the competition.

You may want to look over the competition songs before deciding on your costumes. Also, some of you may want to use some props with your performance. In fact, you may want to use different sets of props for each of your songs."

"We need to break for lunch," suggested Dr. Rob. "After lunch, I will review your lists and try to find some songs that all of you like to be used for the future competition. I can assure you that each of your number one songs will be included in the competition. I will post the songs that will be used along with practice times and locations for each of your groups. We will start practicing tomorrow morning. Unless you have some more questions, then let us break for lunch."

So, everyone went over to the dining hall for lunch. Professor Wogglebug, Dr. Rob, the Scarecrow, the Wizard, Dorothy, Katie and Tommy all sat together. Katie and Tommy told everyone about the morning's activities. Katie had successfully read the second reading book to Dorothy. It was another Wilbert the Pig adventure. Tommy had finished learning the sounds of the consonants and was working on letters and letter combinations that produce the same sound such as: 'c' and 'k,' 'ch' and 'sh,' 'f' and 'gh,' and 'f' and 'ph.'

Katie added that Dr. Rob had been requested to repeat the musical instrument demonstrations again tomorrow. Professor Wogglebug was glad to hear that so many students were showing an interest in music.

It was decided that Tommy and Katie would go practice their reading, writing, spelling, and phonics after lunch. Dorothy would oversee their activities.

Dr. Rob would go over plans for the quartet and quintet practicing. He made a two o'clock appointment to practice his reading with the Wizard and the Professor.

Dr. Rob went back to the music room. He read over the lists of songs and selected the first choice from each list. He had to add in two second choices to bring the number of songs up to five, because some songs made the top of more than one list. In the end, he had selected five songs for the quartets and five songs for the quintets. Two songs made both lists.

It took a while, but Dr. Rob was able to locate ten copies of each of the eight songs. He placed half of these copies on his desk and planned to place the other half on the top of the piano on the stage.

Next, Dr. Rob tried to set up a practice schedule for the ten groups. Each group got a half an hour practice time, each morning.

One half of them would work with Dr. Rob in the music classroom every other day. On days when they were not working with Dr. Rob, the Scarecrow offered to help them practice on the stage. The groups were also encouraged to practice by themselves at least once a day.

Dr. Rob posted the song list and practice schedule on a bulletin board outside the classroom. He then dropped off the copies of the music at the stage and went looking for the Scarecrow. He thanked the Scarecrow for the offer to help with practicing and told him about the schedule and locations of the practice sessions. The singing groups would begin practicing tomorrow.

It was now time for Dr. Rob to go practice reading.

Chapter 21 -- Dr. Rob Reading Lesson

Dr. Rob found the Wizard and Professor Wogglebug in the Professor's office. "Hello!" said Dr. Rob.

"Hello!" replied the Wizard. "Are you ready to practice reading?"

"Yes, I am!" replied Dr. Rob. "I am looking forward to this practice. What do I do first?"

"The first thing you are going to do is to read your old first grade reader book to me again," began Professor Wogglebug. "After that, I will give you another word recognition test."

"But why do all that again?" asked Dr. Rob. "That is what we did yesterday."

"It takes doing the words over and over before you really master them," said the Wizard. "You have to keep reviewing the words or you will shortly forget them."

"Well, if it is really necessary," said Dr. Rob, "then let's get started." Dr. Rob was able to read his old first grade book without any problem. He also got most of the words of the recognition test correct on the first try. After three times through the test, he was able to recognize all the words correctly.

"Now I am going to ask you to read this new first grade reading book," said the Professor. "Except for a few new proper names, it includes the same words as your old first grade book."

Dr. Rob started reading the words out loud. He found it very difficult. When he came to the name, George, he had no idea of how to pronounce it. Professor Wogglebug helped him with the word George. Dr. Rob then read the entire sentence again.

"Why is this so difficult to read?" asked Dr. Rob. "You said it contains the same words as my old book except for some proper names."

"You had the old book memorized, Dr. Rob," said the Wizard. "This new book is not the same story. You can't depend on your memory to help you with the words. Now you are being forced to actually look at each word. It is harder work then just recognizing the old story."

"Oh dear!" remarked Dr. Rob. "You were right. Learning to read is going to take a lot of hard work. Do you really think I can still learn to read at my age?"

"Of course you can still learn to read at your age," said Professor Wogglebug. "If you have the will to want to read then you can learn to read. The stronger your will, the easier and faster you will learn to read. It is really up to you!"

"Now let's try having you look at small groups of words independent of the story," continued the Professor. "The words may or may not make sense together. You are just to read the words to me."

So the Professor held up a flash card containing the words: Run, Toto, run.

Dr. Rob read correctly, "Run, Toto, run."

Next the Wizard held up a flash card containing the words: Run, Toto, run. See Toto run.

Dr. Rob read this correctly as well.

Professor Wogglebug then held up a flash card with the words: Run, Tito, run.

Dr. Rob read the words as, "Run, Toto, run."

"That's not correct," said the Wizard.

"It says, 'Run, Tito, run,'" added the Professor.

"But you tricked me!" exclaimed Dr. Rob. "That is so close to what I said. Besides, I am not sure that even makes sense!"

"You tricked yourself," replied Professor Wogglebug.

"You need to stop depending on your old memories and start looking at each word carefully!" stated the Wizard. "If you don't look carefully, then you brain assumes what is there from your past experiences. Now let's try that flash card again."

So Dr. Rob read the card as, "Run, Tito, run." He was much more cautious about assuming what word he was looking at. He did very well on the rest of the testing.

"Okay, Dr. Rob," said the Professor. "Let's give you a chance to use your memory again. I believe this is the second reading book you used in first grade?"

"Why yes it is!" replied Dr. Rob. "Oh that book brings back some memories."

"Very good!" continued Professor Wogglebug. "Now would you see if you can read it to me?"

Dr. Rob started reading the words from memory. Then he stopped and started over. This time he pointed to each word as he recalled the words from memory.

When he had finished the first chapter, the Professor asked him to read it again. This time he was to say each word twice.

"That's very good," said the Wizard. "How are you with the second chapter?"

Dr. Rob continued working with the book for over an hour. Next, Professor Wogglebug gave him another word recognition test. It was hard, exhausting work. But Dr. Rob continued to apply himself with great vigor. Finally the time was almost up for the day.

"I think it may be time to give Dr. Rob some phonics lessons," suggested the Wizard. "That would help Dr. Rob to pronounce new words when he runs into them."

"That's a good idea," agreed Professor Wogglebug. "We can get Tommy to help him learn to use the computer program for learning phonics. If Tommy teaches Dr. Rob the phonics rules, then Tommy will reinforce his own learning of phonics."

"Does the computer have a vocabulary list for the first grade on it?" asked the Wizard. "If it does, then Tommy could help Dr. Rob pronounce some of the new words."

"Why yes, the computer does have vocabulary lists on it," responded the Professor.

"But I have never used a computer," objected Dr. Rob.

"That's okay, I am sure Tommy will be happy to teach you about computers," replied the Wizard. "He and Katie did a very fine job of teaching Dorothy to use computers. Please don't worry about the computer. You don't need to know much about a computer to run a single program."

"Tell me, Dr. Rob," said the Professor. "How have you been practicing your reading between our sessions?"

"Do I need to practice in between sessions?" asked Dr. Rob. "Why?"

"Because the more you practice reading, the faster you will learn to read!" said the Wizard. "You need to take advantage of every reading opportunity."

"When I was gathering up music for the quartets and quintets to use, I did have to read song titles" replied Dr. Rob. "By then my reading pill had worn off. Making out the music practice schedule wasn't easy."

"Did you practice reading the words of the songs?" asked the Professor.

"Well, I already know the words of the songs," replied Dr. Rob. "But, no! I didn't think about practicing reading the words of the songs. That would have given me a chance to learn to read some new words. I'll have to go read those songs when I am finished here!"

"Now that's the spirit!" replied the Wizard. "You could also start looking at the other notes on the bulletin boards. Every little practice helps!"

"So can we continue these lessons again tomorrow afternoon?" asked Dr. Rob.

"I think we can arrange that," replied the Professor and Wizard together.

"We will also talk to Tommy and see when he can help you with the phonics and vocabulary programs," added the Wizard. "You will find those programs are fun to use. Once you know how to use them then you can practice whenever you like for as long as you like. You won't need to have me, the Professor, or Tommy there with you."

"Well, I will trust you about the computers," said Dr. Rob. "Right now, I am going to go look over that sheet music and see what the words really look like. Then I am going to practice reading the notices on the bulletin boards. I am sure that will keep me busy until dinner time. Thank you for all the help with reading. I just wish I could learn faster!"

"You must remember to be patient," said Professor Wogglebug. "You can learn to read. Just keep doing what you have already been doing. You will be surprised at how many words you will recognize. But it will take time before you can expect to completely understand the notices on the bulletin boards.

"You two have a good day," said Dr. Rob as he left.

Chapter 22 -- The Music Director Lessons

The next day, everyone got up, got dressed and had breakfast together as usual. This included reading and spelling pills. It was time to announce the plans for another day.

Dr. Rob asked, "Professor Wogglebug, would you announce that there will be held beginning music conducting lessons at ten o'clock this morning, in the music classroom. And don't forget that I will be demonstrating the musical instruments again right after breakfast."

The Professor was only too glad to make the announcement.

"Dr. Rob," asked Katie. "Do you think it would be all right if Tommy and I attend the music conducting lesson?"

"I am sure that would be fine," replied Dr. Rob. "I'll see you in the music classroom at ten o'clock."

So, everyone went about their separate ways. Tommy went to practice phonics and spelling rules at the student computer center. He learned that if one has more than one person, place, or thing then one must add an s to the end of the word to make it plural. If the word ends in 's,' 'x,' 'z,' 'ch,' or 'sh,' add an 'es' instead of 's'.

Katie went with Dorothy to practice her reading skills. They reviewed the second book that Katie had borrowed from the Professor. It was another Wilbert the Pig adventure story. Next, Katie started reading a third book. It was the first book of a new series of books about the adventures of a girl that was Katie's age. The star was called Posey Gates.

Dr. Rob went to the music classroom. Here Dr. Rob gave the second musical instrument demonstration. This time twice as many students came to the demonstration than came to the first demonstration.

The musical instrument demonstration was still going on at ten o'clock, when Tommy and Katie arrived at the music classroom. They found a line of students outside the classroom waiting for the music conductor lessons to start.

"Hello, Dr. Rob," said Tommy as he entered the classroom. "Is it time for the music conductor lessons?"

"Well, yes I guess it is ten o'clock already!" replied Dr. Rob. "Are there many students waiting for the music directing lessons? We only announced the lessons this morning."

"Yes, there are a large number of student waiting in the hallway," replied Katie. "Why don't I invite them to come into the classroom?"

"Please invite them in," responded Dr. Rob. "We were just finishing the music instrument demonstration." So Katie invited the students to come into the room.

"If you will all take a seat," said Dr. Rob. "We will get the music conductor lesson under way in a couple of minutes!" Dr. Rob then finished the musical instrument demonstrations.

"Good morning ladies and gentlemen," said Dr. Rob to the students in the music conductor lessons. "Music conductors direct group singing, bands, and orchestras. They may be called upon to give music lessons.

Today, we will learn about directing group singing. This looks easy to do. You saw me directing group singing at the sing-along. Professor Wogglebug, the Wizard and Dorothy, each directed a single group for the round singing at the sing-along. You also saw me acting as a music director when I conducted the quartet and quintet demonstrations.

Now I am sure that all of you know that a music conductor waves their arms around. You might have even seen cartoons where a director started chasing a flying bug while trying to direct an orchestra. Of course the orchestra went wild, trying to follow those directions. It made for a funny story.

Some of you might think that there isn't any organization behind the movement of the director's arms. That the director moves their arms any way they wish. That's not true. It only looks unorganized to those not familiar with directing music. As you will soon find out, there is a definite motion required for directing music.

If one is just conducting group singing, one uses their right hand to help the group keep in time or synchronized with the music. That is the whole purpose of the arm movements.

The left hand can be used to hold a song book. It is also possible to use the left hand to control the volume of the singing.

We will start our conducting lesson by looking at the following sheet music." Dr. Rob proceeded to pass out copies of sheet music to each person present. It was for the song: 'Twinkle, Twinkle Little Star.'

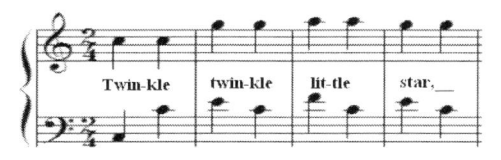

"This sheet music has a musical staff running across the page. It is made up of five horizontal lines. At the beginning of the first line of the musical staff, you will see the treble clef. Some music has two connected musical staffs with the words of the song written in between them. In that case, the bottom staff usually has a bass clef at the beginning of it. To the right of the clef are listed any sharps or flats in the music. Next, is the timing signature for one measure of the song," began Dr. Rob. "This establishes the rhythm of the song. Common values are 4/4, 3/4 and 2/2 timing. Our music has 2/4 time. The top number is how many of a particular length of note make up a measure of the music. The bottom number is the type of note. The measures of the music are separated by vertical bars on the musical staff. We will start by teaching you how to conduct 2/4 timing."

"The top two of the 2/4 timing says there are two notes per measure," continued Dr. Rob. "The bottom four of the 2/4 timing says the notes are quarter notes! 2/4 timing is kept by starting with your right hand raised. Then simply move the right arm down for the count of one and back up for the count of two. Also associated with the timing is the tempo of the music. This determines how fast or slow the beats are to be counted. You repeat the motion for each measure of the music."

"Now if you will all stand up and do as I do and we will practice the 2/4 directing," said Dr. Rob. So all the students stood up and practiced 2/4 directing with Dr. Rob for several minutes.

"Okay, you can sit down," said Dr. Rob. "Conducting 2/2 is similar to 2/4 timing only it is slower."

"Now if you will all stand up and do as I do and we will practice the 2/2 directing," said Dr. Rob. So all the students stood up and practiced 2/2 directing with Dr. Rob for several minutes.

"Okay, you can sit down again," said Dr. Rob. "Conducting 3/4 timing is slightly harder. In this case, you move the right hand down for the count of one, diagonally up and out for two, and diagonally up and back to the starting point for three. Once again, you repeat the motion for each measure of the music."

"Let's all stand up again and try doing 3/4 timing," suggested Dr. Rob. All the students stood up and followed Dr. Rob in practicing 3/4 music directing.

"The last timing we will try today is 4/4," stated Dr. Rob. "Conducting 4/4 timing starts once again, with your hand raised. The hand moves down for one, diagonally up and out for two, all the way across to the left for three, and diagonally up and right to the starting point for four."

"Once again, let us stand up and try directing 4/4 timing," said Dr. Rob. All the students stood up and followed Dr. Rob in practicing directing 4/4 music timing. After several minutes, they all sat down again.

"Now, I know that some of you have seen music directors use both hands when directing a band, choir, or orchestra," said Dr. Rob. "By now you should be wondering what they are doing with their left arms."

"Both arms can be used to get the attention of the singers or players," said Dr. Rob. "For example, you can raise both arms to tell the singers to get ready to sing or play. Bringing the arm(s) down, starts the singing and playing.

The left arm can be used to work with a person or small group of people separate from the main group. The director simply points to the person or small group with his left hand. If the left hand is then raised, palm up, it signals for an increase in the volume. If the left hand is lowered, palm down, it signals for a decrease in the volume."

"That is enough theory for this lesson," concluded Dr. Rob. "Now it is time for us to get out some sheet music and practice directing of singing. We will start by having you watch me direct the singing. I will keep my directions very simple. Then each of you can try directing the singing. Okay?"

Everyone thought that was a good plan, so Dr. Rob got out a stack of sheet music and handed out a copy of it to each student.

"For now, we just need to practice singing this song until all of you are familiar with it," said Dr. Rob. So the group spent ten minutes singing the first verse of the song over and over again.

When Dr. Rob was satisfied that the group knew the song, he began the directing lessons.

"This time, I want all of you to concentrate on the movement of my hands," explained Dr. Rob. "I want you to follow my commands. Before you can be a good director of music, you need to know how to follow the directions of another music director." So Dr. Rob raised his hands and waited for everyone to be quiet and get ready to sing. When he brought his arm down for the first beat of the song, about half the students started singing.

Dr. Rob waved his hands back and forth across his chest to stop the singing. All but two of the students stop singing at once. The other two students stop singing once they realized that they were singing by themselves.

"As I said," began Dr. Rob. "I want all of you to keep an eye on my hands. Let's try it again."

So the students and Dr. Rob continued practicing following and directing the singing until lunch time. By then, many of them could direct simple group singing.

"That's enough practice for today," said Dr. Rob. "We can continue our lessons tomorrow afternoon. We will need a student director for each of our quartets and quintets groups. If you are interested in doing that, see me after lunch."

After lunch, Dr. Rob had ten students visit him. They wanted to be directors for a quartet or quintet. This was all the directors he needed for those singing groups. He assigned a student director to each group and told the directors when their groups would practice.

Meanwhile, Tommy was working on spelling rules in the student computer laboratory. He was learning how to change the tense of a regular verb from the present tense to the past tense by adding an 'ed' to the end of the word. There was one special case of a word which has one syllable, one vowel, and ends in one consonant. In that case, double the last consonant before adding 'ed' to it, unless the consonant was a 'w' or an 'x.'

Katie spent the afternoon reading to Auntie Dorothy. It was a Posey Gates adventure.

At three o'clock, Dr. Rob worked on his reading with the Wizard and the Professor. After an hour of reading practice, the Wizard and Professor Wogglebug took Dr. Rob to the student computer laboratory. Tommy was waiting for them. The Professor showed Tommy the vocabulary lists for different reading grades.

Tommy and Dr. Rob spent the next hour working on vocabulary and phonics.

Chapter 23 -- The Athletic College Organizes an Orchestra

The next day, Dr. Rob held try outs for musical instrument lessons. He wanted to form a small orchestra from the music students. Once again, students were lined up out in the hallway waiting for the try outs.

"Come on in," said Dr. Rob, to the students in the hallway. "We want to give all of you a chance to learn to play the musical instrument of your choice. In addition, we hope to form a small orchestra and give a simple concert in two months or so. If everyone will gather around me, we can get started."

So the students came into the music classroom and gathered around Dr. Rob. He counted twenty-two students. Now he needed to figure out how to arrange them into a small orchestra.

"Learning to play a musical instrument requires constant practice," said Dr. Rob. "It may even be hard work in the beginning. After you get the fundamentals down, you will begin to have fun while you continue to practice and learn. You may even look forward to the days when you can entertain yourself with music that you make up on the spot."

"I am going to show you how play a particular instrument," began Dr. Rob. "Next each of you will get a chance to try to play that instrument. We will repeat this procedure for every instrument that I have here in this classroom. This will give you a chance to decide on what musical instrument you want to learn to play. If there are no questions, then we will start with how to play the triangle." There were no questions.

Dr. Rob picked up a triangle and demonstrated how to play it. Next he got out four more triangles and had the students take turns trying to play them. The students found that triangles were easy to play.

They moved on to the cymbals. "While the cymbals look easy to play, there is a trick to playing them," said Dr. Rob. "You will need to use glancing blows like this." Then Dr. Rob demonstrated the correct way to use the cymbals. He passed out several sets of cymbals for the student to try playing.

Once again, all the students were successful with the cymbals. They found playing the cymbals much more fun than playing the triangles.

Dr. Rob progressed on to the bass drum. He used large drum sticks to keep time on the drum. Next, the students all tried out the bass drum. All the students found the drum easy to beat.

The next instrument was the snare drum. "I must warn you that beating a snare drum is difficult," began Dr. Rob. "You need to hold these small drum sticks loosely, otherwise you damp out the very sound you are trying to produce." He proceeded to demonstrate how to play the snare drum. The snare drums gave many of the students problems. Dr. Rob took note of which students did well with the snare drum.

Dr. Rob demonstrated the drum set to all the students and then invited those students who were good with the snare drums to also try out the drum set.

The last percussion instrument they tried was the glockenspiel. After Dr. Rob demonstrated the glockenspiel, all the students were able to play it to some extent. Once again, Dr. Rob wrote down which students did well.

"Now we will try out the brass wind instruments," said Dr. Rob. "You have to blow into the mouth piece of the instrument with your lips buzzing like this." Dr. Rob demonstrated how to make one's lips buzz.

"You can change the tone of the note by moving these values up and down," continued Dr. Rob. Next, he proceeded to play the trumpet, trombone, French horn, and sousaphone.

Most of the students had trouble making tones come out of any of the brass instruments. Dr. Rob took special note of the few students who were successful at playing tones on these instruments.

"Let's try playing the stringed instruments next," continued Dr. Rob. "I will tune the instrument for you and adjust the bows. You have to put pressure against the strings as you draw the bow across them." Dr. Rob demonstrated the how to play the violin, cello, and bass fiddle. Many students did well with at least one of the stringed instruments. Dr. Rob wrote down these student's names and which instruments they played best.

The last string instrument to be tried was the harp. Dr. Rob demonstrated how to pluck the strings of the harp and followed it with the playing a short song on it. Several students looked promising on the harp. Dr. Rob made notes of this fact again.

"The last group of instruments we will try now are the wood winds," said Dr. Rob. "With them, you have to make this wood reed vibrate to make the tones. We first soak the reeds in water to make them flexible. Next, we put the reed into the mouth piece of the instrument and play it like this." So Dr. Rob demonstrated how to play the clarinet and saxophone. Some of the students tried these instruments. A few of the students were successful at getting tones from the instruments, but they didn't seem to like the instruments. Never-the-less, Dr. Rob took note of who they were for future reference.

Next, Dr. Rob demonstrated the playing of a flute. "You have to blow across this little hole as if you were blowing across the opening in the neck of a pop bottle," said Dr. Rob. "That will produce a tone. The pitch of the tone can be changed by working these values or keys." Dr. Rob played the flute. Several of the students were able to play tones on the flute. Dr. Rob took note of who these students were.

"The final instrument, we are going to try today is the piano," said Dr. Rob. "Any one of you can play a note on it by simply pressing one of the keys on the keyboard. You can all try it for yourself. Now, for those of you who are interested in it, I will let you each play the harmony for a duet with me playing the song, 'Chop Sticks.'"

Many of the students played a few notes on the keyboard of the piano. Finally four of the students were willing to try and do the duet with Dr. Rob. Dr. Rob took notes on which these students were.

"Well that's it for instruments at this time," said Dr. Rob. "Now that all of you have had a chance to try out the instruments, I need to know which instruments you would be interested in learning to play. So come on up here and line up in front of me. I'll ask each of you which instrument or instruments you want to learn to play."

Dr. Rob got students to show an interest in playing the following instruments. They were: two piano players, four drummers, four violinists, four cellists, two bass fiddle players, four trumpet players, two trombone players, four flutists and two harp players. He was able to talk two other students into learning to play the glockenspiel. So he wrote down all the students names and which instrument they were going to play.

"I am going to pass out and assign musical instruments to each of you," said Dr. Rob. "You should always practice using that particular instrument. You will need to learn to tune it properly and clean it. I will hold you responsible for its condition. Take care of it as if it were your own instrument! Let me know if you have any problems with it."

Dr. Rob handed out the proper instrument to each student. The two piano players would have to share the pianos, one in the music classroom and one on the stage.

He proceeded to set up a practice schedule for the lessons for each type of instrument. Each orchestra player was to practice once a day in a group with the other players of the same type instrument. In addition, they were to practice on their own, daily.

Finally, all the members of the orchestra were to get together once a day and learn how to function as a group. They needed to learn to keep in time with the other players. They all had to learn to understand the motions that Dr. Rob made as he directed the orchestra. In addition, they all had to learn to pick out their part from the musical score used by the orchestra. It would mean a great deal of work for each member of the orchestra.

"We will be performing a short concert in a couple of months or so," said Dr. Rob. "We'll be lucky if we can play three simple songs by then. It will be just for fun and to get you use to performing in front of an audience. Hopefully, we can get other students interested in our new music program at that time."

"All of you can leave now, except for the brass wind instrument players," added Dr. Rob. "We want to get you folks started on making good tones on your instruments. The rest of you should be sure to show up at your appointed practice times."

Dr. Rob worked with the brass wind instrument players for another hour. Finally, it was lunch time.

Chapter 24 – Time for a Break

Dorothy, Katie, and Tommy met Dr. Rob as he was walking toward the dining hall. It was a beautiful day.

"Hello, Rob," said Dorothy. "It is such a nice day, I think we should stay outside and enjoy it. Let's go on a picnic."

"Well, I am very busying with music and reading lessons, right now," replied Dr. Rob. "Do you think we could have the picnic some other day?"

"I think Dr. Rob has been working too hard," added Tommy. "He could use a break from all that work!"

"We have all been working hard too!" added Katie. "I think we all need a break."

"That is three for and one against the picnic," counted Dorothy. "I guess we are going on a picnic. Just follow me to the carriage over at the athletic field. Ozma and the Sawhorse are waiting for us with a picnic lunch."

"What about my reading lessons and my music students?" asked Dr. Rob.

"The Wizard and the Professor are going to take care of your music lessons for the afternoon," replied Dorothy. "You can practice your reading this evening."

"You win!" said Dr. Rob. "Let's go on a picnic." So Tommy, Katie, Dorothy, and Dr. Rob headed for the athletic field. Here they met Ozma and the Sawhorse. Everyone got aboard the carriage and the Sawhorse headed down the road that led to the Yellow Brick Road.

"Where are we going?" asked Dr. Rob. "I hope it isn't too far, because I am hungry."

"We are only going a short distance," replied Ozma. "I thought we would hold the picnic at the Park of Peace."

"I remember the Park of Peace," remarked Tommy. "We visited it on our first trip to Oz."

"Didn't it have an enchanted pond in it?" asked Katie. "We met Auntie's goldfish and turtle there!"

"Yes, it does have an enchanted pond in it and you did meet my goldfish and turtle there," replied Dorothy. "Who can say what or whom we will meet there today?"

"Oh goodie!" replied Katie and Tommy, together. They were ready for the picnic.

It took just a few minutes for the Sawhorse to reach the Park of Peace. He pulled the carriage into the park and stopped it next to some picnic tables.

"I don't remember there being any picnic tables here," said Tommy as he climbed down from the carriage. The others followed Tommy's example.

"Well, we didn't bring the Wizard along with us," answered Dorothy. "So we need the tables for our lunch area. Last time the Wizard made us a picnic pavilion out of a handkerchief."

"I think the tables will work out just fine," added Katie. "Maybe we can get Dr. Rob to bring the picnic basket over to the tables?"

"I would be happy to," responded Dr. Rob. He got the basket from the back of the carriage and carried it to the tables. "This is a beautiful park. Can we look around it?"

"I think we should eat first," said Dorothy. "After all, I think Tommy is starving."

"Well, I am sure I could eat a little something," said Tommy. "Don't worry Dr. Rob. We all want to look around the park. But I think the food should come first."

Dorothy and Katie set the table for lunch. Tommy and Dr. Rob filled a pitcher with cool, fresh water, from a well next to the picnic tables. Everyone sat down at the table.

"If you will tell me what you want to eat," said Ozma. "I'll get it for you from the basket!"

"You mean we can have anything we want to eat?" asked Dr. Rob.

"That is just what I mean," replied Ozma. "What will you have, Dr. Rob?"

"I would like a nice ribeye steak, a small lobster tail, and a baked potato with plenty of butter," responded Dr. Rob. "The steak should be cooked medium rare. May I also have some lima beans and a glass of ice tea?"

"No problem!" replied Ozma. "Will that be sweet or unsweetened ice tea?"

"Make it sweet ice tea," replied Dr. Rob.

Ozma reached into the magic picnic basket and pulled out the items for Dr. Rob. He took the plate and tasted the food. Everything was delicious.

Ozma fill the orders of everyone at the table. Finally, everyone started eating. After the main course, everyone had a dessert of their choice. It was a very good meal!

"I enjoyed that meal," said Dr. Rob. "But there is one thing I missed at this picnic."

"What is that?" asked Ozma.

"There weren't any ants or insects," replied Dr. Rob. "Usually about the time one is ready to eat a picnic lunch, the bees and yellow jackets come out to eat. Of course there are always ants!"

"We don't have to have all the bad things at our picnics in Oz," responded Dorothy. "Now you know that you are not in the outside world."

After lunch, Tommy and Katie ran over to the pond. They were looking for fish! Dr. Rob, Dorothy, and Ozma followed them to the pond.

A dog came up behind them and barked a hello.

Dorothy turned around and found Sigi, her mixed breed dog. "Well, hi Sigi," said Dorothy. "What brings you here?"

"Arf! Arf!" replied Sigi and wagged his tail.

"Well, it is nice to see you too," continued Dorothy. "I hope you are enjoying your stay at the Gilbert's."

"Arf! Arf!" said Sigi and he ran over to Tommy and Katie.

"Hi Sigi," said Tommy as he patted Sigi on the head. "Nice to see you are doing fine staying with our folks."

"Tommy," said Katie. "Is that a goldfish?"

"No, it isn't," answered Dr. Rob. "That is a tropical fish. Look! There are more of them over there. That's strange. If I didn't know better I would think that was one of my angel fish."

Just then an angel fish came over to Dr. Rob. "I was right," said the fish. "He doesn't know if we are his fish or not!"

"Well, what can you expect of someone that hardly ever sees us except for feeding us," replied another angel fish.

"Wait a minute!" exclaimed Tommy. "Angel fish live in salt water, right!"

"That's right," replied Dr. Rob.

"Well, last time we visited this pond, it had goldfish in it," said Tommy. "Now I know that goldfish live in fresh water."

"Tommy!" said Ozma. "Remember where you are. This is the Land of Oz. The pond can have both fresh and salt water in it at the same time if I wish it to."

"Tommy!" cried Katie. "Isn't that Auntie's red and white goldfish, called Lady, over by that rock?"

"I guess it is," responded Tommy, as he ran over to the rock. "Hello, Lady!"

"Hello, Tommy!" said the goldfish. "I was wondering if you could find me some shrimpettes."

Katie and Tommy looked behind several rocks until they found the box of shrimpettes. These they fed to the goldfish. It seemed that all eight of Auntie Dorothy's goldfish were there.

Tommy and Katie also found a box of tropical fish food. They handed the box to Dr. Rob. He fed his tropical fish.

Next, Dorothy and the others walked around the park and looked at all the decorative plants and flowers. Everyone was able to find his favorite flowers in bloom. The time of year made no difference to these flowers. They were in bloom all year round.

When the group got back to the picnic tables, they found squirrels and rabbits begging them for food. Tommy, Katie, and Dr. Rob took turns feeding the animals. The animals were so tame that everyone was able to pet them. Some deer also came by for some free food. All the animals were very polite and said thank you for the food.

What was really unusual about feeding the animals was that during all of this, Sigi sat next to Dorothy and didn't make any noise. Normally, Sigi would have been chasing the animals all over the park.

Dr. Rob and the others all had a nice relaxing afternoon. None of them even thought about reading or music lessons. Finally, it was time to pack up the picnic basket and return to the college.

By the time the Sawhorse had the carriage back at the college, it was time for dinner. Dorothy and the others thanked Ozma and the Sawhorse for the picnic and waved goodbye to them.

They had dinner at the dining hall. The Wizard and Professor told them how the music lessons went. After dinner, Dr. Rob and Tommy went to the computer laboratory to work on vocabulary and phonics. They worked on how each vowel had two different possible sounds, a short vowel sound, and a long vowel sound. A vowel says its name when it is used as a long vowel sound!

Later, Dr. Rob met with the Professor and the Wizard so they could all work on Dr. Rob's reading. They were trying to finish the work on his first grade reading books.

Tommy worked on his spelling. He was learning how to make a word plural by adding a 's' to the end of it. However, if the word ended in 's,' 'x,' 'z,' 'ch,' or 'sh,' then one adds 'es' to it to make it a plural.

Katie reviewed her third book with Auntie.

Chapter 25 -- The Drum Lesson

Katie was allowed to take drum lessons along with the students from the college. Dr. Rob started the first lesson with a short history on the use of drums.

"You people are interested in playing the drums as a musical instrument," started Dr. Rob. "However, that is not the only thing drums have been used for. Drums can be used for sending messages long distances. They are also important to the military. At present, drums are used to keep solders and bands in step with each other. At one time, they were even used to control the movement of men into and out of battle. . ." The history lesson went on for several minutes.

"Now I want each of you to get out your drum sticks," continued Dr. Rob. "Remember, I want you to keep your drum sticks with you at all times until you have the mechanics of drumming down solid."

"I am going to tell and show you how to hold your sticks for different types of drumming," said Dr. Rob. "Afterwards, we will all try practicing drum together." The lesson continued on for about an hour.

Finally Dr. Rob dismissed the class with a reminder to get some practice in before tomorrow's class. "Remember, you can practice without having a drum," concluded Dr. Rob. "All you need is your drum sticks and a solid surface."

One thing Katie learned from the first lesson was that one is not born knowing how to play the drums. It took hours of practice just to get down the mechanical skills used in playing the drums.

She also had to learn how to keep time as she practiced. This wasn't easy to do when playing the drum set, since her hands and feet were used for other duties. At first Katie learned to keep time by counting out loud. Eventually, she got to the point where she could keep time in her head.

She got to the point where she started walking around saying, 'a one; a two; a one, two, three,' and moved her arms like she was beating on a drum. Katie was merely keeping time with imaginary music in her head. If you didn't know why Katie was doing it, you might think that she was crazy.

Katie was glad she learned that she could practice snare drum beating without a drum. It was also a quieter way to practice than using the real drum. All she needed were her drum sticks and a wooden table or chair. Katie would simply drum on the table or chair.

Learning to read the music was the simple part of the lessons. After many hours of practice, Katie felt depressed. She felt like she wasn't making much progress in learning to play the drums. Katie was still trying to master the basic skills.

"Dr. Rob," said Katie, one day. "Will I ever get to be any good at playing the drum? I mean it just seems to be practice, practice, and more practice. When can I learn to do a drum solo? Will I ever get to the point where I can just play the drums for the fun?"

"Well, I am not sure, Katie," replied Dr. Rob. "You can't try learning a drum solo until you think you can do the basic skills almost automatically. A good musician gets to the point where he only has to work with the music. He doesn't have to worry about how to do each skill. Have you reached that point yet?"

"I don't think that I am that good, yet," said Katie. "But I would like to at least try working on a drum solo part of the time."

"Why don't we see how well you are doing," suggested Dr. Rob. "I'll do a short drum drill and you try and repeat it after me. I guess you could call this exercise follow the leader."

"That sounds like more fun," agreed Katie.

So Dr. Rob got out another drum set and seat down. He started off with some simple work with the drum sticks on the cymbals. Katie then repeated the movement after him. Next he did a few beats on the bass drum. This was followed by a few taps on the snare drums. Katie was able to follow this movement as well.

"That's pretty good, Katie," said Dr. Rob. "You may just have a natural inclination for playing the drums. Now if we can just teach you to be patient. Try these combinations of drum movements and see if you can still stay with me."

So Dr. Rob combined some cymbals work with the base drum. Katie followed along right behind him. Dr. Rob continued to take Katie through the various skill elements used in doing drumming. He kept increasing the difficulty of the work. Finally, Katie wasn't able to stay up with him.

"That's really good, Katie!" said Dr. Rob. "You have learned much more than you realize. Perhaps it is time for you to start working on a drum solo. Let me look over the music we have and I'll find a piece for you. I should have it for you by tomorrow. We can also have you accompany me on your drums as I play a song on the piano."

"That's great, Dr. Rob," replied Katie. "Thank you!" Katie left the lesson feeling like she had really learned a lot about playing the drums. However, Katie knew she still had a lot more to learn.

The next day, Katie got to practice keeping time softly on the bass drum as Dr. Rob played a song on the piano. This was more fun than just keeping time by herself.

Dr. Rob taught Katie to play a drum roll. This could be used to get people's attention for an announcement or the beginning of a performance. Katie learned that drum rolls could also be used to accompany a comedy act!

"Katie!" said Dr. Rob, at the end of the lesson. "I got a drum solo recording for you to listen to. It is a very basic solo, but I think you can enjoy playing it. The first step is for you to listen to the solo over and over."

"Thank you, Dr. Rob," replied Katie, as she accepted the recording from him. "I am sure that this will be more interesting than just practicing the fundamentals of drumming. May I take this with me and let Auntie Dorothy hear it too!"

"Of course you can," replied Dr. Rob. "But do remember to bring it with you tomorrow when you come for your lesson. We can start your practicing the solo at that time. Have a good afternoon."

"I will," replied Katie, as she ran out the door. "Thank you, again!"

Katie went looking for Dorothy. She found Dorothy in her guest quarters.

"Auntie!" said Katie. "I have a recording of a drum solo that I would like to hear. Would you like to hear it as well? If we like it, Dr. Rob says that I can learn to play it."

"Yes, I would like to hear it," replied Dorothy. "We can play it on my tape playing machine." So Dorothy showed Katie how to play the recording on the tape playing machine in Dorothy's quarters. Then they both sat down and listened to it.

When the recording ended, Katie said, "Well, that does sound like much more fun than just practicing my fundamentals of drumming. I believe I can learn to do it."

"If you can play that drum solo well," added Dorothy, "then I know that you have learned a lot about playing the drums. I think that we might even be able to get your parents to let you take drum music lessons."

"I forgot all about my parents," said Katie. "It seems like we have been gone from home a long time."

"Well, don't worry about it seeming like we have been in Oz for a long time," replied Dorothy. "Time here in Oz is not the same as time in the outside world. I am sure we will be getting home soon."

"Now I am pleased to see you take such an interest in your drum lessons," continued Dorothy. "It is nice that you can now work on a drum solo. But do keep up your practice of the drumming fundamentals. And don't forget, we still need to work on your reading each day!"

"I haven't forgotten the reading," replied Katie. "I want to practice reading with you right after dinner. Will that be okay?"

"That will be fine," answered Dorothy.

"In that case," continued Katie. "Can I borrow your tape playing machine for the rest of the afternoon? Dr. Rob said that the first step in learning to play this drum solo is for me to play it over and over again."

"Sure!" said Dorothy. "Why don't you take the player next door to your quarters? Keep it as long as you need it."

"Thank you, Auntie!" replied Katie, as she took the tape player out the door and headed for her quarters.

Katie spent the next hour listening to the drum solo. By the end of the hour, she was trying to follow along with it using imaginary drums.

Chapter 26 -- The Trumpet Lesson

Tommy was allowed to take trumpet lessons with the students. Dr. Rob started the lesson with a short history of the trumpet and other brass wind instruments.

"The trumpet may well have started out as being a hollowed out ram's horn," said Dr. Rob. "This may be one reason that trumpets are called horns. Trumpets were used as signaling devices long before they were used as musical instruments. . ." The history lesson continued for several more minutes.

"Now I want all of you to get out your mouth pieces for your trumpets," continued Dr. Rob. "The first step in playing the trumpet is to warm up your mouth piece. You do this by holding it in your hands and by blowing air through it. When it no longer feels cold to your touch, it is ready to use. So let's all practice warming up our mouth piece."

All the students got out their mouth pieces and started warming them up. This took them several minutes.

"Now remember to warm up your mouth pieces before you use them each time," said Dr. Rob. "Now let's practice buzzing our lips and playing tones on just the mouth piece." So Dr. Rob demonstrated buzzing his lips and then played a few tones on his mouth piece.

The students tried buzzing their lips and playing notes on their mouth pieces. It took several minutes before most of them got the hang of it. Several students tried playing bugle calls on their mouth pieces.

"I see that some of you have discovered the fact that you can play bugle calls on your mouth piece," noted Dr. Rob. "You can also use your trumpet as a bugle. All you have to do is not use the values to change the tone. The better the range of tones that you can get from just your mouth pieces, the better will be your range of notes that you can play on your trumpets."

"Another thing you need to practice is varying the volume of the notes you play on your mouth pieces," continued Dr. Rob. "First, let's see if we can all play the same note on our mouth pieces. Try this note!" Then Dr. Rob blew a single note on his mouth piece.

The students tried to blow the same note. It took five minutes for Dr. Rob to work with each student until they all blow the same tone.

"Very good," said Dr. Rob. "Now I am going to blow the same note. This time I am going to vary the note from soft, to loud, and back to soft." Dr. Rob then blew the note and varied its volume.

"Now let's all try that together," said Dr. Rob. So the students all played the note again. This time they raised and lowered the volume of the note.

"Okay, now students," said Dr. Rob. "Get out your trumpets. I am going to show you how to get it ready to play."

So the students got their trumpets out of their cases.

"First a word of warning," continued Dr. Rob. "Never jam the mouth piece into the trumpet. If you do, you may never get it back out. Of course that would make it difficult to fit the trumpet back in its case."

"Oh wow!" said one of the students. "What do we do then?"

"Then you have to pay someone at a musical instrument repair store to remove the mouth piece for you," answered Dr. Rob.

"Now gently put the mouth piece in the back part of the trumpet," continued Dr. Rob. "Don't tap it into place. Next, you should check the spit value and drain out any water. Now you are ready to warm up your trumpet."

"We have to first warm up the trumpet mouth piece," said one student. "Next we have to warm up the trumpet itself? This is getting complicated."

"It's only complicated when you are first starting out," replied Dr. Rob. "Just be patient. A week from now, this will all seem so easy!"

The first lesson had ended with the students playing the same note that they had practiced playing with the mouth piece. It was much easier to vary the volume when you were playing the whole trumpet, and not just the mouth piece.

"You need to build up your lung power if you are to play brass wind instruments," said Dr. Rob to the students. "You can do this with deep breathing exercises and through active sports, such as running."

"That's it for today," said Dr. Rob. "Remember to practice everything we did today on your own, before tomorrow's lesson."

It took over a week just for Tommy to learn to play the scale. Even at that, his tones were not fully perfected. He was also doing breathing exercises so that he could play a tone longer without running out of breath. Good breathing is very important when playing a brass wind instrument.

The college students had less trouble learning to breathe correctly. However, their tone quality improvement was just as slow as Tommy's.

Of course everyone had to learn to read music and keep time with a foot as they practice.

Trumpet players have to learn to play different length notes. They need to vary the loudness of the notes. For good sound quality, each note needs to be distinct and stop while the values were stationary.

The tone being played is controlled by both the frequency of the buzzing lips and the position of the values. This makes controlling the tone very difficult. The tongue is used to start and stop a tone.

All in all, Tommy was finding out that playing the trumpet was much more complicated than he had imagined. He knew that he could learn to play the trumpet if he just stuck with the practicing.

"Dr. Rob," asked Tommy after weeks of practicing. "When do I get to try and play a song on this trumpet? I mean practicing scales is necessary, but I would like to try a simple song."

"That's understandable, Tommy," replied Dr. Rob. "Let's try doing a very simple song that you already know how to sing. Let's try doing 'Twinkle, twinkle, little star.' We will start by having you try to sing the song." So Dr. Rob got out the sheet music for the song.

Tommy looked at the sheet music and sang the words for the first verse of the song. Next, he looked at the musical notes on the sheet music. It showed chords and four part harmony.

"How do I play all those notes at once?" asked Tommy. "Don't tell me the trumpet can play chords?"

"Well no, the trumpet can't play chords," replied Dr. Rob. "Therefore one can only play one part of the harmony on a single trumpet. If you want to do harmony using trumpets, then you need at least one trumpet for each part of the harmony. Should you wish to play a trumpet solo, then you must just play the melody of the song."

"That's fine!" responded Tommy. "That leaves just one question. Which of the notes represent the melody?"

"For this song, the melody is the second note from the top of each chord," answered Dr. Rob. "We will need to ignore the rest of the notes. First let me play the melody for you on the piano. After that, we can try to do one note at a time. Finally, we will play it at its normal tempo."

So Dr. Rob played 'Twinkle, twinkle little star' on the piano. Next, he played a single note on the piano and then told Tommy what value setting to use on his trumpet. Finally, Tommy played the note. Dr. Rob and Tommy worked their way through the song one note at a time. They repeated the single note work for several passes through the song.

Now Dr. Bob and Tommy worked through the song, two notes at a time. Next, they did four notes at a time. Finally, Tommy was ready to try the whole song at once.

Tommy played all the notes of the song in the correct order. However, he didn't have the tempo up to speed. Even so, he was feeling better about his being able to play the trumpet. It had taken over an hour for Tommy to learn to play the song this well.

"That's pretty good, Tommy!" said Dr. Rob. "Now you need to practice the song on your own. Don't be afraid to sing the song out loud once in a while so that you can hear how it should be played. I am sure that if you will work on the song on your own for a couple of days that you will be able to play it. Let's call it a day as far as this lesson goes. Keep on practicing. But remember, you want to practice doing things correctly. Otherwise you are just reinforcing how to do a thing the wrong way."

"Thank you Dr. Rob," said Tommy. "I can almost hear myself playing that song correctly. I will go practice the song correctly some more after dinner." Tommy left the room feeling much better about himself.

Chapter 27 – Practice, Practice, Practice

The students worked hard at learning to sing harmony and play musical instruments. It took each of them an hour or two of practice each day.

After a week of practice, Dr. Rob announced, "Each quartet and quintet is being assigned a student music director. The director will help synchronize the timing of the singers. They will also be useful when the singing groups practice on their own. After a group has the song down pat, the director can help the group to put individual expression into the song. This will remove the singing from just being mechanical. It will make the singing come alive!"

The singers had to learn many things. They include: learning the words of the songs, learning to enunciate the words clearly, learning the timing of the song, learning the melody, and then learning their own part. Most of all, they had to learn to follow the director's instructions and hand movements.

The singer of the melody was the leader of the group. The melody makes the song unique and recognizable. Singing the melody was the easiest part to learn. The melody must be heard above the harmony parts. All the harmony parts had to keep in time with the melody.

The other singers had to learn to follow the melody. They were to supplement the melody, not overwhelm it. Timing was everything. The singers must sing as a single unit or team. Fortunately, all the organized sport programs at the Athletic College of Oz had prepared the student to act as a team.

"Remember that each singer is important to the quartet or quintet," said Dr. Rob. "Each harmony part adds to the overall performance. While the person singing the melody seems to have the lead, all the singers are important. It is the total performance of the team that will be judged, not the individuals."

"Remember that any costumes and props should go along with the song and not distract from the song," added Dr. Rob. "You have all come a long way. Keep up the good work."

"One more thing," said Dr. Rob. "You don't have to stand still while you are singing. Add some animation to the songs. Use facial expressions. Move your arms. Move about on the stage. Part of a good singing performance includes acting!"

It is very hard for a person to tell how loud he is singing compared to the rest of the group. This is where the Scarecrow, Dr. Rob, and the student music directors were the most help to the singers. They could stand in the back of the room and hear how the parts all fit together. As an additional aid, Dr. Rob arranged to have the singers tape recorded so they could hear how they sounded to other people.

Of course the singing groups were busy planning their costumes and props for the competition. They were all looking forward to the upcoming competition.

The students learning to play instruments didn't have to worry about learning the words of a song. Instead, they had to learn to read the music, learn to tune their instruments, learn to play their instruments, learn how to follow where the rest of the orchestra was in the song. Finally they need to learn to keep time with everyone else and keep an eye on the conductor.

The first combined practice session for the orchestra sounded like total bedlam. No one knew how to adjust their volume to go with that of the other players. The drummers, harpist, and stringed instrument players didn't want to allow the wood winds and brass winds instrument players a chance to stop for a breath of air. They could breathe as they played their instruments, but the wind instruments run on a person's breath. No one paid any attention to the conductor or where the other players were in the song.

Much of the first combined practice session was taken up with how to read the conductors hand motions. "Yes, I know that you need to watch the sheet music as you are playing," said Dr. Rob. "But you also have to keep one eye on me as I conduct. When I raise my hands like this, it means you are to get ready to start playing. When I drop my hand like this, you start playing. On the other hand, if I move my hands sideways back and forth like this, it means that everyone is to stop playing."

After several combined practice sessions, Dr. Rob was ready to have the orchestra start learning to play a simple song. First he played the song completely through on the piano. Next, he had the violinist try playing the melody. After a little practice, he then accompanied the violinists on the piano. Then it was time for the trumpets to play their parts. Finally, by the end of the session, Dr. Rob had the violins and trumpets playing the song together.

It took two more combined sessions before Dr. Rob was able to get all the players playing the song at the same time. While it didn't sound all that great, it was pretty good for such inexperienced musicians. All in all, Dr. Rob was proud of the progress being made by his music students. So he set up microphones to record the orchestra's playing.

"I want you to know that all of you have come a long ways in a short time," said Dr. Rob. "I am going to record your playing of this our first song. Then I will play it back to you so you can hear how you sounded as a group. In a couple of weeks we can play it again and see how fast we are improving. But really, you are coming along just fine!"

So Dr. Rob recorded the orchestra and then played back the recording. The students were amazed at how different they sounded as a whole orchestra. The individual player could not tell how he sounded as a whole when the orchestra was practicing.

After a couple of months of practice, the orchestra had the mechanics of three tunes down fairly well. "You are doing much better," said Dr. Rob. "Now we can start working on adding expression to the tunes. This will be done by slight variations in the timing of a tune. We will work on this individually and as a group. Mainly, all you need to do is watch my hand signals. They will show you when to speed up, slow down, or simply hold an ending note!"

The mood on the campus had changed greatly since Dr. Rob started working with the students on music lessons. Before Dr. Rob came, the students generally simply walked across the campus. Many of them talked as they walked. Some of the students kept time to the music they were listening to on their radios.

Now, you would also see students pretending to direct music as they walked across the campus. Other students were playing imaginary musical instruments. There were drummers, trumpet players, violinist and so forth. Drummers practiced drumming on the fences. Small groups of four or five students walked singing their songs for the upcoming competitions.

After about two months, the singers were ready for the quartet and quintet completion.

"Professor Wogglebug," said

Dr. Rob, one day at lunch. "I think the singers are ready for the competition. It is time to schedule the competition and put up posters advertising it."

"I'm glad to hear that," replied Professor Wogglebug. "I'll be happy to schedule the competition and put up posters. This is Tuesday, why don't we have the competition a week from Friday?"

"That will be great," replied Dr. Rob. "I'll tell the singing students at practice later today."

That afternoon at singing practice, Dr. Rob announced. "We will be having the singing competition a week from Friday. I think you are all ready for it. As a help to all of you, I would like to stage a dress rehearsal for next Monday. This will let you actually try out all of your songs, costumes, and props before the actual competition. You will do everything just as you will on the night of the competition. If need be, you will still have time to make minor changes to your performance before the competition."

The following Monday, all the singing groups met together at the stage. The groups then drew straws to determine the order in which they would perform. Everyone wore their costumes. All the props were ready. The sound and lighting systems were ready for use just like they would be on the night of the competition. This was a closed rehearsal. Once the use of the sound and lighting was explained to everyone, only one singing group at a time was allowed in the stage area. This way, they couldn't judge their performance against the other performances.

All the performers were a little nervous. Some of the groups made little mistakes, as were to be expected. All in all, the rehearsal went well. Dr. Rob was very pleased.

After the rehearsal was over, Dr. Rob gathered all the groups together and said, "You did very well for a rehearsal. I think you should all be proud of yourselves. You will still get to practice for four more days. Have a good performance!"

Of course Dr. Rob, Katie, and Tommy were still practicing their reading, phonics and spelling.

Chapter 28 -- The Singing Competition

The student quartets and quintets had been practicing faithfully for two months. Dr. Rob, the Scarecrow, and the student music directors worked very hard to bring each group to its peak.

Finally, the big day of the competition arrived. People came from all over Oz to hear the competition. A group of Fuddles had come to hear the competition. They were trying very hard to stay together. Miss Cuttenclip had brought a large clear plastic box full of her paper dolls to watch the competition. The box would keep the dolls from being blown over by the expected applause. Even Her Majesty, Ozma II was present.

The singing groups were to compete in three categories: singing style, costumes, and audience response. The judges were, Dr. Rob, the Wizard, the Scarecrow, and Her Majesty. An applause meter was used to measure the audience response.

Katie and Tommy were to use drum rolls and trumpet fanfares to announce each group. When everything was ready, Dr. Rob walked up to the front of the stage and asked, "Katie, may I have a drum roll?" So Katie played a drum roll to get the audience's attention.

"Ladies and Gentlemen, it is my pleasure to announce the beginning of our singing competition," announced Dr. Rob. "Before we start, we wish to thank the Emerald City Style Shop for finishing all the costumes for the performers, tonight."

"Tommy may I have a trumpet fanfare?" asked Dr. Rob. So Tommy played a trumpet fanfare. "The first groups to perform tonight will be the Beauty Shop quintets. Each quintet will sing the same five songs."

"The first Beauty Shop quintet to perform will be the Munchkin Beauties, and here they are now!" said Dr. Rob. The Munchkin Beauties came on to the stage to a welcoming applause. They were dressed as beauty contestants. Their stage set was the runway of a beauty pageant. The Munchkin Beauties sang their five songs. At the end of their performance, they received loud applause. The people from Munchkin Country really liked the performance.

Dr. Rob had Katie play another drum roll and then had Tommy play a fanfare. "And now, ladies and gentlemen," announced Dr. Rob. "Let me introduce the Winkie Stylists." The Winkie Stylists all wore the latest fashions and hair styles. Their stage set was the runway of a fashion show. Each singer showed off her outfit. They receive a welcoming applause and then sang their five songs. Once again, there was loud applause at the end of the performance. The people from Winkie Country really liked the performance.

Once again, Katie played a drum roll and Tommy played a fanfare. Then Dr. Rob announced, "And now we have the Gillikin Hair Dressers." The Gillikin Hair Dressers came on stage dressed as beauticians and customers. Their stage set was a beauty salon. Once the applause died down, they performed their five songs. Of course they receive loud applause. The people from Gillikin Country thought the performance was great!

With a drum roll from Katie and a fanfare from Tommy, Dr. Rob announced, "Last, but not the least of the Beauty Shop quintets, it is my privilege to introduce the Quadling Debutantes." The Quadling Debutantes came on stage wearing white ball gowns. They looked stunning! Their set was a ballroom. Each Debutante had a male escort. Once the applause died down, they song the five songs. The applause was louder than ever. Of course the people from Quadling Country loved the performance.

Once things quieted down, Katie gave another drum roll and Dr. Rob announced. "That was the last of the Beauty Shop quintets. Now it is time to hear the Barber Shop quartets. They will be singing two of the same songs as the Beauty Shop quintets used, plus three new songs."

Katie gave a drum roll and Tommy gave a fanfare. "And now I give you the first Barber Shop quartet, the Munchkin Farmers." The Munchkin Farmers came on the stage dressed up as Munchkin farmers with the boots and pointed hats with pom-

poms on the rims. Their stage set was a barnyard with a hay stack in it. The four singers were pitching hay with pitch forks. Once the applause stopped, they sang their five songs. After they finished singing, they receive a standing ovation. The folks from Munchkin Country enjoyed the performance most of all. Dorothy applauded loudly.

Katie gave a drum roll, Tommy played a fanfare. "Now it is time to introduce the Winkie Foresters," said Dr. Rob. They came onto the stage in Tin Woodman outfits. The set was a forest of trees. The Foresters were working on chopping down a large tree. They received a loud welcoming applause. Once things got quiet, the Foresters sang their five songs. When they ended their performance, they receive loud applause. The people from Winkie Country really enjoyed the performance. The Tin Woodman gave the loudest applause.

With a drum roll and a fanfare, Dr. Rob announced the next group, "Ladies and gentlemen, I now give you the Quadling Magicians." The Quadling Magicians came on stage dressed up in Wizard of Oz outfits. Their stage set was bare except for a large table in the middle of the stage. The Magicians gathered back of the table, they placed their hats on the table and began pulling rabbits out of their hats. When the applause died down, they sang their five songs. Once they were finished, they got a loud applause. The folks from Quadling Country really enjoyed the performance. The Wizard of Oz gave them loud applause.

Katie gave a drum roll, Tommy sounded a fanfare, and Dr. Rob said, "Now let me introduce the next singing group, the Gillikin Sorcerers." The Sorcerers came on stage dressed as mad sorcerers. They receive a loud applause. The stage set looked like a sorcerer's workshop. The singers were moving around, working on a magic spell. Once the applause died down, they sang their five songs. At the end of their performance, they receive loud applause. The citizens from Gillikin Country really enjoyed the performance. Glinda the Good gave then loud applause.

Dr. Rob introduced the last Barber Shop quartet with a drum roll and a fanfare, "And now the last of the Barber Shop quartets is the Emerald City Singers." They came on stage to loud applause, dressed as bakers from the Emerald City Bakery. The stage set looked like the donut bakery area of the Emerald City Bakery. The singers threw donuts to the audience. Once the donuts and applause ran out, they sang their five songs. The group received a standing ovation. The college students loved the free donuts! Ozma enjoyed their singing.

Finally, Dr. Rob introduced the last singing group, the only mixed quintet. "And now I give you the mixed quintet, known as the Oz Mixed Singers," announced Dr. Rob. The Oz Mixed Singers were wearing the costumes of the five regions of Oz. The stage set showed a May pole. The singers were dancing around the May pole weaving together five colored streamers. When the applause ended, they broke into singing their five songs. When the songs ended, they received a standing ovation. All the students gave them loud applause.

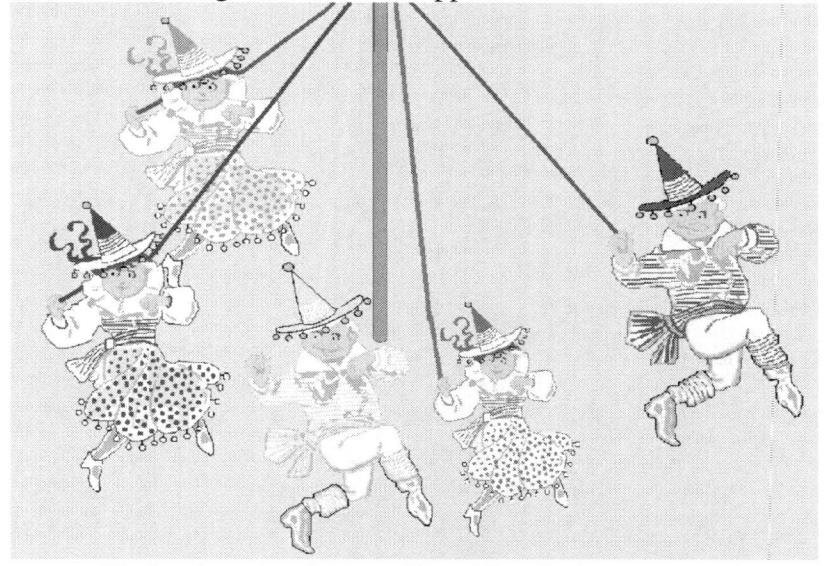

Katie played a drum roll and Dr. Rob announced, "That was the last group of the last category. The winners of each category will be announced shortly." Then the judges got together and compared notes.

Five minutes later, Katie played another drum roll. Dr. Rob announced, "The winner of the Beauty Shop quintets was the Quadling Debutantes. The winner of the Barber Shop quartets was the Emerald City Singers. Now, the Quadling Debutantes, the Emerald City Singers and the Oz Mixed Singers will have a sing off. Each group will sing the same two songs. This time, there will be no stage settings."

The audience grew quiet and the Quadling Debutantes performed. Next, the Oz Mixed Singers performed. Finally, the Emerald City Singers performed. "Be patience for a couple of minutes and we will announce the overall winner," said Dr. Rob.

The judges got together once more. After several minutes they had made their decisions.

At this time, Katie played a drum roll and Tommy gave a fanfare. "The winner of the overall competition is the Oz Mixed Singers," announced Dr. Rob. "It demonstrated the most vocal range in singing. It had the most variety and colorful costumes and the biggest audience response. Let's give the winners a big hand!"

The singing contest was followed by a sing along for all present. This made for an enjoyable ending to a great evening. Refreshments were served.

The Fuddles enjoyed the evening so well, that they forget to stay together and went all to pieces. Fortunately, Tommy and some of the students were able to quickly put them back together.

Everyone congratulated Dr. Rob and all of the students that took place in the contest for a job well done. Dr. Rob insisted that he couldn't have done it without the help of the Scarecrow. Many students made inquires about the new Music Program and how they could get into it.

Her Majesty made the suggestion that the singing competition become an annual affair. She offered to have a trophy made up for the competition. Everyone agreed that this was a very good idea.

The next day, Dr. Rob and the winners of the singing competition traveled to China Country and put on a performance for the Princess and Her subjects.

Chapter 29 -- The Orchestra Concert

The month after the singing competition, the college orchestra was ready to give its first concert. Even with the addition of the Scarecrow on the triangle and the Tin Woodman on the cymbals, it was still a very small orchestra. All the players were very nervous about giving their first concert.

Each student had practiced the instrument lessons at least once a day. For the last month, they had also put in an hour a day working on several orchestra songs. The good news was that even though no one was a great instrument player in their own right, the group effort was much better than any individual effort.

Finally, Dr. Rob was willing to have the orchestra give a very short concert. At lunch one day, he talked the idea over with, Dorothy, Katie, Tommy, and Professor Wogglebug.

"I want the orchestra to give a concert," said Dr. Rob. "But I only think that they can play three songs. We need some way to make the concert longer."

"Why don't you have the winner from the singing competition do a song or two?" asked Katie.

"That's a good idea," replied Dr. Rob. "How about you two each do a solo for us as well?"

Dorothy said, "That's a great idea. It will give you two a chance to work on your stage fright."

"My stage fright is fine," replied Tommy. "But I don't know if I am ready to do a solo."

"She means it will give you a chance to overcome your stage fright," added Katie. "I'm with you brother. I don't think I am ready for a solo."

"Oh sure, you are," replied Dr. Rob. "If you can just remember what you sounded like when you first started playing your instruments, you would know that you have improved tremendously. Besides, doing a performance is part of learning to play a musical instrument."

"I'll tell you what, Tommy," said Dr. Rob. "I'll be with you on the stage and accompany you on the piano. That will keep you from being alone, and the two of us will sound better than only one of us."

"Well, if you are sure no one will laugh at me, then I will give it a try," said Tommy.

"I guess I can try to do my solo too," added Katie.

"Good!" said Dr. Rob. "Professor Wogglebug, would you set up a time for the concert?"

"How about next Friday night?" replied the Professor.

"That sounds fine," replied Dr. Rob. "Now remember, this concert is just for fun. Let's all try to enjoy yourselves. I'll see you later, right now I want to go find the Mixed Oz Singers and let them know about the concert." So everyone went on about their own business.

At orchestra practice that afternoon, Dr. Rob announced, "You all have come a long ways on working as an orchestra. This Friday night, we will give a short concert of our three best songs. The Oz Mixed Singers will also sing several songs. And Katie and Tommy will perform as well."

"What will we wear?" asked a student.

"The men will wear black suits and ties, with white shirts," replied, Dr. Rob. "The women will wear long black dresses. Remember, we want to have the audience's attention on our music, and not our outfits. Are there any other questions?" There were no other questions.

"Okay then," said Dr. Rob. "From now until the concert, we will practice as an orchestra on the stage. We want to get used to playing as we will for our concert."

Everyone practiced hard for the rest of the week. When Friday came, they had one more nervous practice on the stage in the morning. "This is our last practice before the concert," said Dr. Rob. "After we finish it, please try to relax for the rest of the day. Get a little rest. Eat a little extra at lunch. Then have a light dinner. I will see you all here, one half hour before the concert."

So everyone took the afternoon off from practicing and try to relax. By concert time, the dining hall was packed with spectators. They had come from all over Oz. Once more, Her

Majesty, Ozma II was in the audience. Of course, Miss Cuttenclip came with some of her paper dolls. The Fuddles were also present.

Dr. Rob had all the drummers give a drum roll, to get the attention of the audience. "Ladies and Gentlemen," began Dr. Rob. "It is my pleasure to introduce to you the new orchestra for the Athletic College of Oz." The audience broke out into applause. When the applause stopped, Dr. Rob continued speaking, "This is the first concert for the orchestra. It is just a practice concert. We will only be playing three songs. In addition, we will have Katie playing a drum solo, Tommy playing a trumpet solo, and the Mixed Oz Singers will be singing. After the performance, we will have a sing along."

Dr. Rob took his place and raised his hands. The orchestra came to attention and prepared to play. He dropped his hands and the orchestra played 'Twinkle, Twinkle, Little Star'. This was followed by two other simple songs.

The orchestra sounded fantastic. When they finished the third song, the audience gave them a long applause. There were requests for an encore.

"We can repeat these songs again if you like," said Dr. Rob. "But first, let's have Katie, Tommy, and the Mixed Oz Singers do their performances." This got another loud applause.

Katie gave her drum solo, accompanied by Dr. Rob. It was another musical hit, with much applause. Katie was really glad that the performance went so well.

Tommy then gave his trumpet solo, accompanied by Dr. Rob. He was nervous, but it went well. He received more applause.

The Oz Mixed Singers then did their performance. When they were finished, there were cries of encore. The Singers did two more songs.

Dr. Rob then had the orchestra play their three songs again for the audience. At the end of the last song, they receive another standing ovation.

"That is all the prepared music that we have for you tonight," announced Dr. Rob. "You have been a good audience.

It was a pleasure performing for you. Now we will have our sing along."

The sing along lasted for another hour and one half. Everyone present had a good time. At the end of the sing along, refreshments were served.

Tommy was ready for the refreshments. He enjoyed them. Now that the performance was over, Tommy was no longer nervous. Katie and the orchestra players were also feeling much better now that they had finished performing.

More students were requesting information on the new music program from Dr. Rob and Professor Wogglebug. All the performers were receiving praise and many questions. The performers were enjoying being popular.

"You did a good job with the orchestra," said Dorothy, to Dr. Rob. "Katie, you did a great drum solo. Tommy, you were great on the trumpet."

"Thank you," replied Dr. Rob. "The students all did great!"

"But you got them to do it," added Professor Wogglebug. "You have really done a good job at starting the music program for the college."

"Thank you, but I had a lot of help," insisted Dr. Rob. "The Wizard, Dorothy, Katie, Tommy, the Scarecrow, and you Professor, all helped me to do the job. And of course, I couldn't have been successful without all of the students!"

"Never-the-less," added Ozma, "Her Majesty, Ozma II was favorably impressed with your work. She asked me to pass along Her congratulations."

"Okay," agreed Dr. Rob. "I did work hard on your music program. I am happy that it is doing so well."

"It is I who must thank all of you for helping me to start learning to read," added Dr. Rob. "I never would have believed it would be possible for me to learn to read after so many years. It will change my whole outlook on life. Thank you."

"Katie and I also thank you for helping us with our spelling and reading problems," added Tommy.

"And we were all happy to help Dr. Rob," added Katie.

"Okay, then," summarized Dorothy. "We all are thankful for each other's help! Come on, let's have some more refreshments."

The following day, Dr. Rob and the orchestra visited China Country and did another performance.

Chapter 30 -- Familyworld

Dr. Rob, Tommy, Katie, Dorothy, the Wizard, Glinda and the Scarecrow were gathered together with Ozma in Ozma's sitting room. Ozma had just served tea and cakes. Everyone was congratulating Dr. Rob for his work on the Music Department for the Athletic College of Oz.

"The orchestra's concert really stirred up the students' interest in learning to play musical instruments," said the Professor. "How did you teach them to play that well in such a short time?"

"Well, I can't take all the honors," replied Dr. Rob. "The music pills furnished by Professor Wogglebug really helped speed up the mental skills used in playing musical instruments. I also had very dedicated students. I just wish all my music students would work as hard as your colleges students did for me."

"The singing competition was also a big hit," said the Scarecrow. "I am glad I got to help out with that."

"I really needed your help, Scarecrow," answered Dr. Rob. "Thank you for helping."

"Dr. Rob," said Ozma. "I would like to give you this little certificate in honor of your work on our music program. Would you like me to read what it says?"

"I think I would like to try reading it for myself," replied Dr. Rob, as he accepted the certificate from Ozma. "In big letters at the top, it says: 'Athletic College of Oz.' Next, it says: 'presented to Dr. Rob Patterns, in recognition of his work on setting up the music department.' And look here! It is signed by Ozma the II, ruler of Oz, and Professor Wogglebug. That was very nice of Her Majesty!"

"She was only too glad to do it for you, Dr. Rob," responded Ozma.

"Of course you realize that you can't show this certificate to anyone," said Tommy.

"Why not?" asked Dr. Rob.

"Because everyone will think you are crazy," responded Katie.

"This is especially true for adults," added Dorothy. "For some reason, adults don't think they should believe in the Land of Oz."

"Well, you may have a point there," agreed Dr. Rob. "Never-the-less, I will treasure it always. Thank you for all your kindness. Oh! And I am very thankful that you helped me see the advantages of being able to read. I will contact one of the groups you suggested as soon as I get back to Kentucky."

"The Wizard told us that you have completed your second grade reading books," said Dorothy. "That is very good progress. It looks like you can learn to read!"

"Yes, you were right," said Dr. Rob. "I can still learn to read even at my age. Thank you for helping me out!"

"We were all glad to help you," said the Wizard.

"If you think you are ready to go on to Familyworld?" enquired Ozma. "Then it is time for everyone to say good bye."

"I have one question," said Dr. Rob. "What will happen to the college music program once I leave?"

"The directors of the Royal Court Band and the Imperial Cornet Band of Oz have offered to teach the courses," replied Ozma. "Some of the band members offered to help with music lessons. Don't worry, the music program will continue."

"Thank you, that takes a load off my mind," said Dr. Rob.

"Good bye, Dr. Rob," said everyone at once. "We will see you in Eastern Kentucky."

"Good bye, everyone," responded Dr. Rob.

Ozma spoke, "Glinda and Wizard please arrange for Dr. Rob to be placed on the airplane shown on his ticket."

The Wizard left the room and returned with what looked like the outside door to an airplane restroom. Glinda performed a spill and a red fog formed around the door.

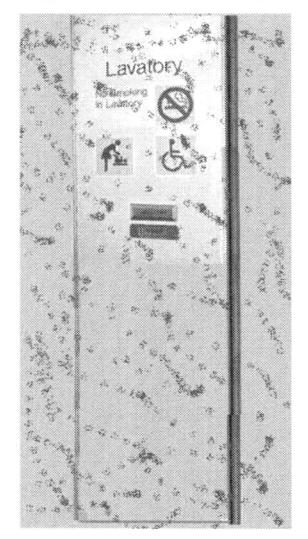

"Dr Rob," said Ozma. "Glinda is an expert in making time wrap holes. That door leads to one that will take you back in time to a rear restroom on your plane to Familyworld. When you are ready just open the door and enter the restroom. Lock and unlock to door and you will find yourself on the airplane flight printed on your ticket."

"Thank you for everything," replied Dr. Rob. He entered the restroom and shut the door. The red fog disappeared.

"Show us Dr. Rob," said Ozma to the Enchanted Picture on the wall of the sitting room. At once, Dr. Rob appeared in the picture, seated on an airplane.

"That doesn't look like our airplane," said Tommy.

"It isn't our airplane," added Katie. "Our airplane has a blue interior. This airplane has a red interior."

"It seems Dr. Rob has finally gotten on the right airplane," replied Dorothy. "I hope his trip to Familyworld is successful."

"I am sure he will have an enjoyable time performing Eastern Kentucky folk music," replied Ozma.

Dr. Rob had found his seat a back seat of the airplane. No one noticed his sudden appearance. Dr. Rob looked around the cabin of the airplane. It had magazines, pillows and other thing scattered about on the floor. So this airplane must have also gone through some turbulence.

After several minutes, the pilot announced that the airplane would be landing in Orlando, Florida shortly. Dr. Rob's airplane landed a few minutes later at the Orlando airport.

The other members of his group were there to meet him at the airport.

"Boy are we glad to see you!" said one member of the group. "You won't believe what we have been going through. What have you been up to?"

"But why were you worried?" asked Dr. Rob. "Why all I have been doing for the last few hours is riding the airplane from Lexington to here."

"Well, you know how you sometimes show up at the wrong time, or day, or place for a meeting," replied another member of the group. "So we decided that we better check with the airline to see if you caught your airplane."

"And guess what the airline told us," continue another member of the group. "They said that you checked in on time all right, but that you didn't board the airplane. Can you imagine that? We thought you might have gotten on the wrong airplane."

"Well, a few minutes later, we doubled checked again with the airline. Now they said you did get on the airplane after all. Now how are you going to explain that?"

"Why that is easy to explain," replied Dr. Rob. "All of you know Dr. Dorothy Gale, Professor of Psychology."

"Yes we do," replied the group.

"Well, I accidently got on the airplane to Familyland instead of Familyworld," continued Dr. Rob. "Dorothy and her nephew and niece were going to Familyland on that airplane. We all sat together on the airplane and it flew through some rough weather. So we took a side trip to the Land of Oz, where we helped to put together a Music Department for the Athletic College of Oz. Then they had me placed back on the right airplane for Familyworld. And here I am!"

"Right!" replied the group. "It sounds like something that Dorothy might say. We can believe that you got on the wrong airplane. But there is no way that we will believe you transferred from one airplane to another airplane in mid-air. Surely you didn't think that we are going to believe your story? And of course we know that you as an adult don't believe Dorothy's stories about the Land of Oz."

"The only magical kingdom we believe in," added another member of the group, "is the magical kingdom of Familyworld. We know it is real. We can see and touch it for ourselves!"

"I only said it was easy to explain, not that it was easy to believe," answered Dr. Rob. "Would it be easier to believe that the ticket agent punched the wrong information in to the airline computer? Later the agent corrected the mistake."

"Now that is more believable," said the first member of the group. "Anyway, we are glad to see you. Come on, let's go get your luggage and get you to the Hotel."

The next day, Dr. Rob and the group got to rehearse their act at the Folk Music Center. After they were satisfied with their performance, they took the rest of the day off and toured Familyworld. Of course they tried out many of the rides. They enjoyed themselves like a group of young boys.

Dr. Rob visited a gift shop and brought himself some children's books. He was going to read the stories about Snow White, Cinderella, and Robin Hood. If anyone asked him about the books, he could say they were for his nephews and nieces.

He went back to his room and looked at the books. The pictures in the books helped him to follow the stories. There were a few words he didn't understand. Maybe he could ask Dorothy about the words when he got home.

The following day, they gave their first performance to a stand up crowd. There were people from many different nations in the audience. It was very successful show. The highlight of the show was the dueling banjos song, done by Dr. Rob and one of his fellow professors.

Dr. Rob and his group did six performances a day for two days. After they had finished their engagement, they were invited to come back again in the future. It was a pleasant experience for the entire group.

Chapter 31 -- Familyland

Dorothy, Katie and Tommy spent the day visiting old friends in the Emerald City. They went to Emerald City Style Shop and saw the latest fashion for the Land of Oz. They enjoyed lunch at McTodd's Hamburger Stand.

Rodeo Willy and Calico Sally dropped by the palace. They helped Tommy show Katie some tumbling. Rodeo Willy helped Katie learn how to stand on her head.

Tommy and Katie practiced their spelling and reading. Finally it was time for them to leave the Land of Oz. They went to Ozma's quarters, where Ozma, the Wizard, Glinda and the Scarecrow were waiting for them.

"I want to thank you for your help in setting up the Music Department at the college," said Ozma. "Now it is time for you to continue with your vacation."

"Well, we enjoyed helping Dr. Rob setup the Music Department," said Dorothy.

"We learned a great deal about music while we were helping Dr. Rob," added Tommy.

"Right!" added Katie. "Now at least Tommy moves his arm in time with the music when he pretends to direct music. However, I think he needs more practice before he can play a trumpet."

"Well, your drum playing could use a little work too!" said Tommy. "I think we both need to take music lessons before we try playing music for our friends."

"We did enjoy just getting to try out all the instruments," said Katie.

"We need to thank all of you for helping us find out about the causes of Tommy's and Katie's problems with spelling and reading," added Dorothy. "All in all, it was a useful visit to the Land of Oz."

Dorothy, Katie and Tommy said good bye to everyone.

Ozma asked the Wizard and Glinda to return Dorothy, Katie and Tommy to their flight to Familyland just after it exited the storm. The Wizard brought in the outside airplane restroom door. Glinda performed a spell and a red fog formed around the door.

"Katie," called Ozma, "you need to enter the restroom and lock the door by sliding the latch in the door. That will turn on the lights. Then unlock and exit the restroom back into your airplane. Tommy and Dorothy will follow you once you leave the restroom. Here is what the inside of the door and the latch look like. Enchanted Picture show us the inside of the door."

The picture showed the door. Tommy pointed out the latch to Katie. Katie entered the restroom.

The Enchanted Picture showed Katie.

Katie looked around the very compact restroom. She was glad she didn't need to use it. Katie exited the restroom.

Tommy and Dorothy repeated what Katie had done. The red fog disappeared.

"Enchanted Picture," said Ozma. "Please show us Katie, Tommy and Dorothy."

The Enchanted Picture changed to show Dorothy, Katie and Tommy back on their airplane flight to Familyland. They had the same seats as before, but this time, Dr. Rob wasn't with them.

"Wow!" said Tommy. "That was some storm we went through. I didn't think an airplane ride could be such fun!"

"Speak for yourself, brother," said Katie. "My stomach doesn't need any more fun like that. Well, at least not until we get to try out some of the rides at Familyland."

"Well, I am glad the storm is over," added Dorothy. "It is also nice that we finally got Dr. Rob on the right airplane. Now we can get on with visiting Familyland. Of course we will also work on your spelling and reading!"

"I now know that Katie was right!" said Tommy. "The 'ie' and 'ei' spelling rule does use the word 'weigh', not 'way'. Now I need to work on past tenses of irregular verbs."

"Well, we can practice spelling for a few minutes each morning while we are vacationing," said Dorothy. "We will have to find some computer programs to help you when we get home. You should also write in your journal every day."

"Right!" replied Tommy. "I can do that at night, just before I go to bed. Of course I will take notes during the day."

"You almost make spelling and reading sound fun!" said Katie. "There is hope for you yet, brother. Maybe I can read to you at night, Auntie? You could take it as a bed time story."

"Yes, Katie, that would be nice," replied Dorothy. "After we get back home, we will have to get you a public library card. I am sure our local library will have many books that you will enjoy reading."

"You mean they will let me have my own library card?" asked Katie excitedly. "That sounds like fun!"

"I am sure your parents won't mind if you get a library card," said Dorothy. "In fact, I am sure they will be delighted. The librarian can help you find books at the right reading levels. You may find out that reading is a very enjoyable way to pass time."

"And I am sure you two will enjoy school more in the fall, if you overcome your spelling and reading problems this summer," concluded Dorothy. "School and learning can be fun when you succeed at what you are doing."

"Won't our parents be surprised when we tell them what we are doing about our problems," said Tommy. "We couldn't have made these plans without your help, Auntie."

"Yes, Auntie," added Katie. "Thank you for encouraging us to work on our problems."

The rest of the flight to the Orange County airport was without any more incidents. The airplane landed and taxied to the Jet Way. Dorothy, Katie, and Tommy got off the airplane and found their luggage without any problems. They took a limousine to the Familyland Hotel. Their room was ready when they arrived at the hotel.

It was dinner time by Tommy's, Katie's and Dorothy's internal clocks. So Dorothy took them out to the dining room of the hotel. After dinner, they visited the hotel gift show.

Dorothy made Katie and Tommy buy postcards to send to their parents. She also bought Tommy a small notebook and a mechanical pencil that he could carry with him. Dorothy bought a book for Katie to read.

Katie and Tommy wrote messages to their parents on the postcards. It told about their safe arrival and that Dorothy was helping them plan working on their reading and spelling problems.

Tommy then got the pad of paper out of his suitcase which had his journal entries in it. He spent an hour trying to write about the trip so far.

Katie got out the new book that Dorothy had just bought her. She then began to read it to Dorothy. The book was about the adventures of a raccoon.

When Tommy had trouble with spelling of some word, Dorothy would help him. When Katie had trouble with the meaning or pronunciation of a word, Dorothy helped her.

Everyone was tired from the long trip. They decided to call it a night. So they all got ready for bed. Tommy and Katie were almost asleep before their heads hit the pillows.

The next morning, they got up, got dressed, and had breakfast sent up to their room. This was Katie's and Tommy's first experience at using room service. After, breakfast, they all went to Familyland.

Tommy took good notes on what they did. This included all the rides they rode and the shops they visited. At one shop, Dorothy bought some books on fairy tales. They ate food all day long at the park.

When they got back to their hotel room, they were tired. However, Dorothy still had Katie read her one of the fairy tale books. Katie selected the story of Cinderella.

While Katie was reading, Tommy was writing in his journal. He wrote about all the shops on Main Street. He really liked the old automobiles that he got to ride in.

The next two days were spent in a similar fashion. By the time the vacation was over, everyone was worn out. The three of them slept most of the time on the flight back to Eastern Kentucky.

George met them at the airport. "Hello, everyone," greeted George. "I hope everyone had a good time?"

"We had a wonderful time," replied Dorothy.

"I had a great time," said Tommy. "We got to meet Auntie Dorothy's friend, Dr. Rob of the college Music Department. Father, can I learn to play the trumpet?"

"It was a very fun trip," added Katie. "May I learn to play a drum set?"

"We'll have to see what can be arranged," replied George. "But first you need to improve your spelling and reading. After that, I will support you even if you want to form your own drum and bugle corp."

When they got to their car, Sigi was waiting for them. He had spent his vacation with George and Tammy, the parents of Katie and Tommy. Sigi was happy to see Dorothy.

George drove Auntie Dorothy home. Everyone helped Dorothy carry her luggage inside. Then Tommy, Katie and George went home. Katie and Tommy had many things to share with their parents.

Will Katie improve her reading? Will Tommy improve his spelling? Will both of them get to take music lessons? The answers to these questions are yet to be told.

Made in the USA
Charleston, SC
05 July 2012